8-11

W
Savage
Wind river

c.1

WIND RIVER

OTHER FIVE STAR WESTERN TITLES BY LES SAVAGE, JR.:

Fire Dance at Spider Rock (1995); *Medicine Wheel* (1996); *Coffin Gap* (1997); *Phantoms in the Night;* (1998); *The Bloody Quarter* (1999); *The Shadow in Renegade Basin* (2000); *In the Land of Little Sticks* (2000); *The Sting of* Señorita *Scorpion* (2000); *The Cavan Breed* (2001); *Gambler's Row* (2002); *Danger Rides the River* (2002); *The Devil's Corral* (2003); *West of Laramie* (2003); *The Beast in Cañada Diablo* (2004); *The Ghost Horse* (2004); *Trail of the Silver Saddle* (2005); *Doniphan's Thousand* (2005); *The Curse of Montezuma* (2006); *Black Rock Cañon* (2006); *Wolves of the Sundown Trail* (2007); *Arizona Showdown* (2008); *The Last Ride* (2008); *Long Gun* (2009); *Shadow Riders* (2009); *Lawless Land* (2010)

WIND RIVER

A WESTERN DUO

LES SAVAGE, JR.

FIVE STAR
A part of Gale, Cengage Learning

GALE
CENGAGE Learning

Detroit • New York • San Francisco • New Haven, Conn • Waterville, Maine • London

GALE
CENGAGE Learning

Copyright © 2011 by Golden West Literary Agency.
The Additional Copyright Information on page 5 constitutes an extension of the copyright page.
Five Star Publishing, a part of Gale, Cengage Learning.

LIBRARY OF CONGRESS CATALOGING-IN-PUBLICATION DATA

Savage, Les.
    Wind river : a western duo / by Les Savage, Jr. — 1st ed.
      p. cm.
    ISBN-13: 978-1-59414-947-4 (hardcover)
    ISBN-10: 1-59414-947-X (hardcover)
    I. Savage, Les. No-gun marshal. II. Title.
PS3569.A826W56 2011
813'.54—dc22   2011004257

Published in 2011 in conjunction with Golden West Literary Agency.

Printed in Mexico
2 3 4 5 6 7 15 14 13 12 11

ADDITIONAL COPYRIGHT INFORMATION

CONTENTS

★ ★ ★ ★ ★

THE NO-GUN MARSHAL

★ ★ ★ ★ ★

I

Lee Britt stood in front of Keno Hall on the corner of Douglas and First, feeling the tension that had been building in Wichita ever since the railroad trouble started. That tension was in the miniature Kansas whirlwinds batting down Douglas Avenue from the Arkansas River, in the nervous knots of men that stood talking on the plank sidewalks. There was more to it than the railroad trouble, though. Britt could sense that whenever one of those men cast a furtive glance at his hand.

Unconsciously he raised his hand—the right one. There was a bluish-gray hole in it just below the wrist, puckered, odd-looking. There was another of those holes in his hip, but both wounds were healed now; both were a month old. He was back on the job as city marshal, the job he'd held so many years. Why should this talk be going around?

Diagonally across the street was the New York store. Britt had been stepping off the sidewalk in front of it that night just four weeks ago. He recalled the sudden sensation of danger that swept him with the sight of a blurred shadow between Keno Hall and Ma Mansion's boarding house. As he had stopped there, one foot on the plank walk, one in the rutted street, that shadow had become a man.

It was Ron Dary, lean and cat-eyed, moving into the light with a six-gun in each fist. Even as his hand flashed down, Britt knew he was helpless. Dary's thundering shots caught him, one slug hammering into his hip, spinning him half around. The

11

other smashed his gun hand as he fell. Dary made a half move forward as if to finish the job, but the sudden surge of men through the swinging doors of Keno Hall made him scuttle back into the shadows and disappear.

Lying there with Kansas dust bitter in his mouth, Britt told himself he had been expecting this. Somebody in Wichita was trying to delay the westward movement of the Santa Fe Railroad, was hiring toughs from the Delano district to waylay the Irish labor crews. Britt had begun investigating, knowing that sooner or later the interests who hired the toughs would hire a killer to gun him because he was poking his nose in too far.

The marshal grinned thinly to himself. As yet he only had a faint idea of who was behind it all, but sooner or later somebody would slip. Then they'd be sorry Ron Dary hadn't finished the job that night.

The second floor of Keno Hall was lighting up now, and a dull, methodical voice was calling keno numbers. Dusk gave a square, solid look to Britt's compact figure. The city marshal's badge glinted fitfully on his tan cowhide vest, drawn tautly over the bulk of his shoulders. Dark woolen pants were belted around a tree-trunk middle, and his ivory-handled .45 hung on a hard, driving thigh.

He looked up expectantly as the planks shook beneath a man's boots. His deputy, six foot two and lean as a split rail, was coming to make the evening rounds with Britt. The big Army Model Colt sagging around Tom Moore's narrow hips seemed about to slide down around his ankles, and his horny-knuckled hands, hanging so awkwardly from bony shoulders, looked incapable of having any skill with the gun. Appearances in that case, Britt knew, were very deceiving.

The two men fell silently into step and started across Main Street, headed for the tough Delano district, across the Arkansas

River from the main part of town.

Moore spat into a wheel rut and then cleared his throat before he spoke.

"Folks're sayin' it was Ron Dary who led that bunch of Delano toughs against the railroad gang last week."

"Quite possible," said Britt dryly. "Is that all folks are saying, Tom?"

"Wal, now, Lee," grunted Moore reluctantly, "I guess you know the talk that's goin' round as well as I do. Nerve is a funny thing. Hangs sorta precar'ously 'tween guts and skill. Smash a man's skill, even temporar'ly, an'. . . ."

"And you might smash his nerve too, is that it?"

"Yeah," muttered Moore. "Yeah. There's this new edict you passed 'bout men checkin' their hardware with you while they're in the confines o' town. That ain't like the ol' Lee Britt. Your gun hand was your skill, an' folks're sayin', when Dary blasted your hand, he. . . ."

"He blasted my nerve, too," finished Britt harshly. Then he stopped under the Texas House's ornate overhang, supported by carved white porch posts; a faraway look entered his gray eyes. "I've been thinking about that, Tom. Maybe I shouldn't blame them. Do you realize I can't even be sure myself that Dary didn't smash my nerve until I meet him again, man to man?"

II

Wichita's second cattle season hadn't yet started, but still the town was filling with men who had come to work the rush months—loud men, rough men, tough men. A buffalo hunter padded past Britt and Moore, his Ute moccasins gaily beaded, his braided hair greasy from habitually wiping his hands on it after eating. A bunch of rugged bullwhackers jostled across the Douglas Avenue bridge, flannel shirts and blue jeans covered with stockyard dust.

Jay Clagget's Blue Steer was the largest gambling hall on Delano. Three sets of double batwing doors stretched across its front and they were constantly creaking in and out. Britt pushed through the first set into the smoky rooms. A gilt-framed mirror hung above the long pine bar, and on the bar itself were piled costly pyramids of sparkling glasses. The walls were hung with blue velvet above the six green-topped tables that took on anything from faro to chuck-a-luck or old sledge. A piano tinkled from somewhere to the rear, and the constant buzz of voices had a hypnotic quality. Everything seemed in order.

Britt was looking for Jay Clagget's gray suit among the men, when one voice raised above the others. The marshal moved slowly toward its source. A group of railroad officials stood at the bar, a small space left on either side of them by the rest of the patrons. Britt recognized Will Jarret as the man speaking, a big-beaked, sallow-faced fellow, dressed in a blue frock coat and stovepipe hat. There was a conspicuous bulge under his coat on the right side.

"I tell you," he bellowed, pounding the bar, "that damned city council won't do a thing. I've been up to the courthouse repeatedly, but all they say is . . . 'It's in the hands of Marshal Britt!' And yet these outrageous attacks keep up. Last week a gang was attacked cutting ties and three of them killed."

One of the men laughed nastily. "Britt. That's funny. He might have been some good once. Not now."

"Well, damn it," swore Jarret, "we're bringing in some new crews on the seven P.M. tomorrow and they're gonna be armed with scatter-guns. Anybody tries to waylay em'll find themselves blown clear back to Leavenworth."

As Britt moved forward, the teamsters and stockyard hands opened a path for him.

He spoke flatly. "I see you still pack iron, Jarret. That edict applies to you railroad men as well as everybody else."

Jarret whirled, automatically shoving back his coat with an elbow to reveal the Smith & Wesson holstered beneath. The piano faded in an off-key diminuendo. Buzzing voices trailed into heavy silence.

For a moment Jarret seemed coiled up tight for the draw, his knees letting him down into a crouch, his face setting into determination. Britt stayed almost carelessly relaxed, watching Jarret's eyes as they lowered unwillingly, drawn to the marshal's gun hand, hanging maybe an inch above his white-handled .45. Jarret had been in Kansas long enough to know all about Britt and that ivory-butted gun of his.

It took the railroad man only that one tight moment to decide.

He sagged back against the bar, seeming to be shaken by what he had almost done. With a shuddering breath, he took the gun out, careful to hold it by the barrel. Britt jerked his head toward Moore, half behind him, and Jarret handed the revolver to the deputy. Then he pushed himself away from the bar and shoved through the crowd, head down, still quivering a little. The piano broke into a loud tune; men shifted back toward the green-topped tables.

Tom Moore chuckled in Britt's ear. "You knowed he warn't gonna draw all the time. I can always tell when you got 'em figgered, 'cause you get that squint to your eye."

"Jarret builds railroads," said Britt laconically.

Then he turned to face Rowdy Joe Lowe, thick through the head as well as the shoulders, and the partner of Jay Clagget. The short man came down the bar from where he had watched the proceedings. He had a strange, hoarse voice.

"You sure have Jarret buffaloed. Guess they don't forget the old days, eh, Marshal?"

Moore looked disgustedly at Lowe's heavy gold watch chain dangling across his fancy waistcoat. "What old days? What's any diff'runt nowadays?"

"Never mind," said Britt evenly. "Where's Clagget?"

Though it showed plenty of gold, Lowe's grin was forced. "You're doin' your rounds sorta early, ain'tcha, Britt?"

Britt's voice took on an edge. "I asked you where Clagget was."

Lowe's grin faded. "Why, he'll be around later. I think he went up for a shave."

The marshal's eyes narrowed a little and he nodded curtly, then took a last look around the smoky room. A few men were watching him, speculation in their glances. He might face down a hundred like Will Jarret. There would still be Dary. . . .

Britt and Moore finished their rounds quickly, looking in on aging Kate Sandall's two raucous dance halls, taking a drink at John Beard's Big Table. Everything seemed quiet enough—men couldn't kick up much ruckus without their guns. Back across the bridge, Britt stopped in front of Gould's Barber Shoppe, the only one in town.

"You go on to the courthouse," he told Moore, "and check in Jarret's smoke-pole for him. I think I'll git a haircut."

It was a comfortable chair, none like it between Wichita and Leavenworth, and he settled back with a sigh. "Jay Clagget been in today?"

The barber tested his scissors. "Nope. Ain't seen Clagget fer . . . lemme see . . . last Tuesday, guess it was. Three days."

"Well," murmured Britt, "seeing as how he didn't come in for a shave, you might give me one as well as a haircut."

III

The marshal had always liked to sit on Ma Mansion's front porch, after he ate his lunch at the boarding house, and talk to Del Mansion. The girl put a man at his ease, with her quiet smile and her soft voice. She had a cool look to her, what with the fair hair swept back over a smooth forehead, brightened by a ribbon at the back—not too coolly though, not with that dancing mischief that came and went in her big blue eyes. He felt those eyes on him now as he sat tilted back in a rawhide-seated chair, spurless boots propped on the white porch rail.

"You're still eating with your left hand," she said. "I thought the other was healed."

He felt muscles in his face tighten, and he thought: *Damn it, does everybody have to talk about my hand?* "Now, Del, it'll take a little time to switch back again, that's all."

She leaned toward him impulsively, her face a little pale. "You're going to poke your nose right back into that railroad mess, aren't you, knowing they're out to get you?"

It wasn't his hand she was worried about, he reflected, trying to make his smile easy. "It's my job, Del, that's all."

"Yes, your job," she said bitterly. "And you don't even know who it is you're fighting."

"Now, maybe I do, in a way," he said quietly. "Remember how Abilene mushroomed when the railroad hit it and the Texans brought their longhorns there to ship East? For three or four seasons it was known as the wildest, wickedest town on the American continent. Then the railroad pushed on west to Newton, hit there about July of 'Seventy-One. The bottom dropped out of Abilene. Newton became the wildest, wickedest town on the continent. And so on west to Ellsworth, and Newton dropped from the picture."

She frowned. "But what has that got to do with this?"

He leaned back farther, smiling faintly. "The same thing is happening here. We've had one crazy season. Eighty thousand head shipped East, four thousand carloads. Two or three thousand drunken cowboys spending their money down in Delano and at Keno Hall every night."

Understanding widened her eyes.

"But the Santa Fe's pushing on to Dodge City. If it reaches there before the next season, Wichita will go just like Abilene and Newton and Ellsworth. The boys down at the Blue Steer and the Big Table and Keno Hall must have a tidy chunk of capital sunk in their establishments. I reckon they'd be right peeved if Dodge City took away most of their business, and the only way they can keep it here is by keeping the railroad from going on to Dodge City. I imagine they'd go to some lengths to protect their investments. That's why they're stirring up the cowboys to fight the railway laborers."

"But surely not all of them," she said tensely. "Which ones . . . who?"

"There's a lot of 'em, isn't there?" he said. "Georgie Bangs at Keno, John Beard, Jay Clagget, Rowdy Joe . . . even Kate Sandall. I couldn't rightly say which one."

There was a catch in her voice. "Meanwhile you're liable to get murdered any minute of the day. Ron Dary isn't finished. He's been seen in town."

"Yeah, Dary," he mused. "Why do you suppose he bushwhacked me instead of coming out in the open, man to man?"

"He's been in Wichita long enough to know how good you are. Maybe he's afraid of you."

"That's what I figured," he said. Then he took his boots very carefully from the rail because Jay Clagget and his partner, Rowdy Joe Lowe, were coming down from the river. The short, heavy-set man made quite a contrast to Clagget, dressed as he was in a loud-checked suit and fancy-topped bench-mades, a stogie in one side of his thick-lipped mouth. Clagget had on a gray frock coat, gray pants hanging outside of tan Justins. His white Stetson was conservative if expensive.

Britt's eyes crinkled at the edges as he ignored Lowe and studied Clagget's narrow, rather sardonic face closely. He shouldn't underrate this quiet man whose heavy-lidded eyes held a hint of vicious cleverness.

" 'Afternoon, Miss Mansion," said the gambler, tipping his hat. "And you, Marshal . . . how's the hand?"

Britt tightened a little inside at the edge of sarcasm in the man's too-easy tones. "My hand's all right. I can handle a gun's well as I used to."

Clagget's eyes glittered. "I'm glad to know that. Folks haven't heard you practicing out behind the stables like you always did before. They were beginning to wonder."

He smiled ironically, tipped his Stetson again to Del, then turned and walked on down Douglas.

To Britt, there was an insult in the arrogant swing of his shoulders. Rowdy Joe Lowe laughed hoarsely, then went after his partner, half running to catch up. The marshal followed them with his eyes, thinking of a man and his dog.

"Oh, there you go again," said Del impatiently. "Always studying people. I can tell every time. You get those wrinkles around your eyes."

He answered, but his thoughts weren't on the words. "It helps sometimes. Remember what I told you about Charlie Sanchez? I knew sooner or later he'd come gunning for me, and I knew he was the faster man on the draw. So I began watching him when I got the chance. He had a nervous downward twist to his mouth that'd come a split second before he did anything. Mounting a horse, stepping off the sidewalk, picking up a drink . . . it was always the same, that nervous twitch to his lips, telegraphing what he was going to do. I waited for that when he met me down by the loading platforms. Just a split second, but it gave me the edge. I guess it saved my life."

She laughed indulgently. "All right. And what was so interesting about Mister Clagget? He didn't have a twitching mouth."

"No," said Britt, "nothing so obvious. Clagget's a clever man. And so immaculate. I was wondering what a man like him would be doing with Arkansas River mud on his pants cuff."

IV

It was late that afternoon when Britt turned the corner at Keno Hall and headed up Main Street toward the livery stables, where he was due to meet his deputy. Squinting against the dying sun, he found himself thinking of Ron Dary. A quick, nervous, catty type, Dary. Twenty-five, maybe, and intelligent—intelligent enough to know when to be afraid. As Del had said, Dary had been in Wichita a long time before the railroad, before the Delano district, even before Clagget and the other gamblers. He'd seen Britt's skill with that ivory-butted gun more than once.

When Big Red Daniels had escaped jail, for instance, in 1869, he'd gotten out with a pair of Paterson five-shots and no holsters, so when Britt holed him up in the Texas House, the marshal knew Big Red would have those guns in his hands.

Ron Dary had been in the crowd that had seen Britt go in after Daniels, and he'd been there when Britt came back out, dragging the redhead's dead body.

There was Sanchez, too, down by the railroad. He was a talented, hatchet-faced killer, and rated faster on the draw than Britt. Their gun dives had seemed simultaneous. Yet, when the smoke cleared, it was Sanchez lying in the sawdust by the loading platforms. Dary had seen that, along with the usual crowd who inevitably saw a gunfight. There were other names, too, a long list of them, reaching back and back. Deadly men, swift men, killers. Some of them Britt had studied; some he'd had to meet with only his skill, his hair-trigger draw. Was that why Dary hadn't been willing to meet him in the open?

Britt turned into the gloomy stables, eyes roving to the stall where Clagget always kept his big white mare. The stall was empty, and a faint smile curled the marshal's lips.

★ ★ ★ ★ ★

They rode down First Street to the river, Moore and Britt, and they cantered into the bottomlands, passing southward beneath the bridge connecting Delano with the rest of Wichita. The Arkansas was a broad, sluggish river, its mid-channel islands covered with stunted cottonwoods and scrub pine, looking like dark knobs of fur sticking up out of a rippling, gray-blue blanket.

Britt gave his nervous little pinto its head through the blackjack timber that stretched for miles past the bridge. Behind, saddle creaking with his restless weight, forking a huge red roan, Moore grumbled: "You git the damnedest idees. My hoss is knee deep in this bottom mud already. That cussed shack is prob'ly rotted away by now, anyhow."

Britt laughed a little. "Old Mel Rusket hid out in it when those stock detectives were after him, remember? It'd be right handy for Dary if he wanted to stick around Wichita."

He reined in where some short, gray-green buffalo grass gave footing in the mud and dismounted easily so his leather wouldn't squeak. He ground-hitched his horse and slogged into a grove of hackberries, Moore following. A light evening breeze blew through the leaves, making an eerie, clacking sound. Falling dusk hid the sod-and-timber shack until Britt parted some wild sumac and looked across to where it stood against a high, muddy cutbank.

There were two horses outside, one Clagget's rangy white mare. By the door stood Clagget himself, talking to the lean Dary, their figures hardly more than shadows in the growing dusk.

"I thought so," muttered Britt. "Only I didn't figure Clagget exactly, until I saw that mud on his pants cuffs."

"This must be where he was last night when we made our rounds early," whispered Moore.

"He sure wasn't getting a shave," said Britt.

21

Moore pulled his knees out of the mud with a sucking sound. "And he's the varmint what hired Dary to gun you. He's the polecat hirin' those Delano toughs to tangle with the mick labor gangs. Whut are we waitin' fer?"

He heaved up out of the scarlet sumac, hauling at his Army Model.

At the sound of his slogging boots, Clagget and Dary whirled. The gambler didn't have a saddle gun, and there was no revolver at his hip, but Dary made up for that. He had both big sixes out and was shooting before Moore had taken his third step.

"Tom, wait! It's not time yet!" called Britt.

But it was too late now, and he threw himself after his lanky deputy, knowing that was the only thing left to do. Lead whined past him, snapping through the hackberries behind. Moore pitched onto his face, still firing blindly, jerking a little with the slug in him. Britt stumbled through the buffalo grass, only dimly aware that Clagget and Dary were mounting.

Moore tried to rise, cursing bitterly. "Never mind me, damn it! You can still nail 'em from here."

But the marshal helped him sit up, and Moore looked at him with mingled amazement and pain twisting his long-jawed face.

Then his eyes flashed to the .45 still in Britt's holster.

"Lee," he choked, "you never even drawed your gun."

V

The 7:00 P.M. train had already pulled in when Moore and Britt got back to town. There was a mob of Delano men in front of Keno Hall, holding torches high, seeming to be waiting for something. Yes, waiting for Ron Dary and Jay Clagget. Down by the loading platform was the new labor gang, armed, as Jarret had promised, with ugly-looking shotguns. It would be a bloody tangle.

The marshal rode close to Moore, supporting him in the saddle, and Moore's eyes were filled with accusation. Britt couldn't meet that gaze. Moore had refused to believe the rumors of his smashed nerve; he had been loyal when even Del had doubted, and he felt Britt had let him down back there in the bottomlands. Britt couldn't explain, though—not yet. It left him terribly alone.

Britt slid from his lathered pinto, moving around it to help the deputy down, searching the street for Clagget. He'd ridden hard, hoping to beat them back, because this was the showdown. Clagget's hand was forced. The gambler wouldn't miss stacking Ron Dary up against Britt if he thought Britt's nerve was gone for sure.

The marshal led the two horses to the hitch rack in front of Keno Hall, helping Moore to ease himself down on the plank walk. Blood leaked between the fingers Moore held over his side, and he still watched Britt with that terribly hurt look in his eyes.

Del must have seen them from the parlor window. She came down Ma Mansion's front steps and was suddenly in Britt's arms, sobbing a little against his cowhide vest. He held her for a moment with his hands tight against her back.

She stiffened suddenly, turning a dead white face up to him: "Lee! You can't go out there, not now, not like this. Please, Lee. . . ."

The sullen pound of hoofs came from the bridge end of Douglas Avenue, and Lee gently disengaged her arms. There wasn't much emotion inside him now; he only knew that Dary and Clagget had pulled their horses back onto lathered, mud-splattered haunches, swinging down without yet having seen Britt there near the sidewalk. He moved out farther, something solid and ungiving about his square figure standing there in the wheel ruts of the street.

His voice was deceptively soft, but it carried: "Dary."

The gunman turned; so did Clagget. The crowd spread into a semicircle that blocked the corner of Douglas and Main. Britt wondered if Dary would have pulled iron there in the bottoms had he known the marshal was behind Moore. No matter now, both men had their guns leathered and that made it even.

"No shooting me down from the dark now, Dary." Britt smiled thinly. "I have as much chance as you."

Dary leaned forward a little, cat eyes snapping to Britt's gun hand, the puckered hole still very apparent just beneath the wrist. Was Dary remembering Charlie Sanchez who had been rated faster than the marshal and who had died before the skill of that hand?

Britt took his first deliberate step forward and there appeared those telltale crow's feet at the corners of his gray eyes. Dary's face grew set and pale. Was he recalling how Britt had dragged Red Daniel's body out of the Texas House?

Clagget snarled: "His nerve's broken. *You* broke it. Draw, damn you, draw!"

Britt took his second unhurried step, and back of his acute awareness of Dary was the realization that Clagget was throwing everything into the pot now; his hand was on the table.

Dary rose perceptibly on his toes, mouth thinned to a white-lipped line. Was he remembering those other men who had died before Britt's white-handled gun, deadly men, skillful men, fast men, the list of them stretching far back into Wichita's past?

"Draw," choked Clagget, his sardonic mask gone, his face twisted with rage and fear.

And Britt took that last step, nerve stiffening his gun arm as it had so many times before—only that was no good now. For that instant Dary was stretched like green rawhide, everything concentrated into his coming draw.

Then he seemed to shrivel up. He settled back onto his heels, taking a choked breath. "No, no!" he sobbed suddenly.

Britt reached out his hand. "I'll take your guns, Dary."

Eyes still glued to that gun hand, Dary fumbled for his belt, unbuckled it, handed it over to the marshal. Everybody saw what happened next.

Sweat suddenly broke out on Britt's face; his mouth twisted in a sudden spasmodic reaction to pain; muscles in his neck twitched with a terrible effort of will. And the fingers of his bullet-marked hand began closing around that belt with agonizing slowness. One by one they closed, jerking almost uncontrollably at times. And finally he held the weight of the heavy gun belt in those stiff, white fingers. A gasp of pure torture hissed between his set lips.

With an explosive curse, Clagget moved, like a striking snake. His right arm bent at the elbow—up, down. Britt was looking down the double-barreled bore of a nickel-plated .41 Derringer. The gunshot didn't come from those barrels, though. It came from Ma Mansion's porch, a terrible, thundering detonation.

Clagget jerked his head up in awful surprise. Then he folded to the ground, Kansas dust popping up from beneath his body.

Del stood on the porch, her dad's huge Sharps buffalo gun still wreathed in smoke.

Britt knew he had won. The crowd of Delano toughs wouldn't be any trouble with their backer gone. The railroad gang would have no use for those scatter-guns.

Things seemed to fall apart then. The Sharps clattered to the floor and bounced down the steps. Del followed it, throwing herself into Britt's arms, sobbing, shaken with having killed a man. The marshal felt Dary's heavy gun harness slipping from nerveless fingers.

Del was saying: "I knew your hand was paralyzed when you held me that last time. Your fingers wouldn't flatten. They stayed all hooked and bent, digging into my back."

He remembered how she had suddenly stiffened. "Dog-gone. Guess I forgot in the excitement. I was real careful up to then, though you were the hardest one of all to fool."

Moore was looking at him in weak amazement. "That's why you couldn't draw in the bottoms, why you warn't practicin' out behind the stables like you used to . . . and why you passed the edict 'bout men checkin' in their guns."

Britt nodded. "Couldn't have every Tom, Dick and Harry calling my bluff and making me draw. I had to save my thunder for the showdown . . . and Dary."

"But why, why . . . with a paralyzed hand?" Del asked in a husky voice.

"It's just the way I'm built, I guess," he murmured. "I could have let it out that my hand was ruined. But that wouldn't have solved things. Do you think I could have lived with myself, could have asked you to marry me, thinking that maybe Dary had smashed my nerve, never knowing for sure one way or the other because I didn't have the guts to face him?"

"There was every chance of your being killed," she sobbed.

"Nope," grunted Moore, spitting in a wheel rut. "I think his chances were pretty good. I think he had Dary figured down to a T."

And looking over Del's shoulder at the beaten Dary, standing in a crouch with his fearful eyes flashing from man to man like a cornered rat, Britt thought so, too.

26

★ ★ ★ ★ ★

WIND RIVER

★ ★ ★ ★ ★

I

Just outside of town Frank Ives caught up with the wagon carrying the dead man. It was a mountain wagon with a cut-under front gear, and the home-made coffin was roped in behind the seat so it wouldn't bounce. A gaunt old man was driving and a blonde girl sat beside him, a shabby tartan shawl pulled tightly about her shoulders. There was a pair of outriders, tow-headed young men in patched linsey-woolsey clothes. They both turned to give Ives a suspicious look. He thought it was a pretty hard-scrabble outfit.

His Appaloosa mare had a single-foot gait that took Ives past the funeral wagon and got him into Medicine Lodge a few minutes ahead of them. The Wyoming town wasn't much more than a single main street one block long. There were only two buildings with any glass and one of them had *SALOON* painted on its big window in peeling gilt letters. A group of townsmen stood in front of it, watching the oncoming wagon. Ives pulled to a halt by the curb and spoke to one of the men.

"They told me at Rock Springs that some of the outfits might be hiring here."

"Anchor's the only outfit in Wind River Basin," the townsman said. Without taking his eyes off the wagon, he made a motion across the street. "White-headed jasper in front of the *Clarion* is Tom Russell."

Ives looked toward the two-story clapboard building with a sign over the door: *Medicine Lodge Clarion, Jeff Lee, Editor.* Ives hesitated, unwilling to cross the street. He hadn't thought a town this size would have a newspaper. Then he cursed himself. It didn't matter where he went—there would always be a newspaper.

There were four men standing beneath the sign. Three of them were obviously cattlemen, the white-headed Tom Russell and a pair of his hands. It was just as easy to identify the fourth man as the newspaper editor. The ink stains that no amount of washing would remove had made an etching of every tiny line in his hands. Ives crossed and halted his horse beside the three other animals standing at the rack. He dismounted and turned to Russell. The man was short, paunchy, with legs bowed to a horse-collar shape. Weather had given his face the color of old tobacco and his tufted white brows almost hid his eyes.

Ives said: "Rock Springs said you might need some roundup hands."

Tom Russell didn't answer Ives. He didn't even look at Ives. None of the men did. They were all watching the wagon. It had entered town now and the rattle of its passage was the only sound in the street.

Ives got a closer look at the driver. He was a gaunt, towering man in his sixties, with a face straight from the Bible—burning eyes sunken deeply in their sockets, a wild tangle of gray hair and curly gray beard. The blonde girl beside him had a haunting face, fey, elfin, tilted angles, and secret hollows. As the wagon came abreast of the *Clarion*, the old man drew the team to a halt. The two riders with him checked their horses, letting them fiddle in the dust. The gray-bearded driver settled his baleful eyes on the man to Tom Russell's right.

"You come to give yourself up, Fargo?" he asked bitterly.

The man named Fargo stirred so sharply that his spurs jangled. Ives figured he was somewhere in his middle twenties, tall, alley-cat lean, wearing yellow ropers' gloves and a blanket coat with buckskin patches on the elbows.

"Nobody's giving himself up, Zachary," Fargo said.

The bitter grooves deepened in Zachary's face, and he started to speak again, when something he saw beyond Ives checked him. It made them all turn to look. Ives saw a man coming along the walk from the direction of the nearby jail. He was stubby as a sawed-off shotgun, and looked about as tough. He wore a hard hat and a butternut coat with a sheriff's star on its lapel. He gave Ives a shrewd glance as he stopped. He looked them all over carefully, and finally spoke to Russell.

"You saved me a trip to Anchor, Tom."

"Don't thank me, Doyle," Russell snorted. "We read it in the *Clarion*. Judge Gimble has issued a warrant for Cliff's arrest. We come to see it torn up."

Sheriff Doyle glanced quizzically at the editor. "You jumped the gun, Jeff. Zachary Thayne swore out a complaint against Fargo, but the judge hasn't issued any warrant yet."

Jeff Lee made a sputtering sound and brushed at his longhorn mustaches. They were stained by the same ink that etched his hands. "What's Gimble waiting for?" he asked. "It's open and shut."

"The judge wants to be sure about something first," Doyle said. He was fishing around in his shirt pocket as he spoke, and brought out a copper-cased, bottleneck rifle cartridge. "This was found about a hundred yards from Peter Thayne's body. It's a Spencer shell." He looked at the man with the yellow gloves. "Don't you tote a Spencer, Fargo?"

Fargo wheeled without answering the sheriff and stalked to a tiger-striped roan standing at the rack. From a rawhide scabbard Fargo pulled his saddle gun and brought it back. He snapped down the loading lever and the action ejected a cartridge that hit the puncheon sidewalk with a metal clatter. Fargo stood holding the rifle and staring at Sheriff Doyle with smoldering eyes, making no move to pick up the cartridge. Finally Doyle stooped to retrieve it. The shell was shorter, straight-sided, obviously no match for the bottleneck cartridge.

Russell turned to Jeff Lee. "So that's the airtight evidence your paper was raving about. That bottleneck shell comes from an Indian Model. I doubt if you'll find a gun in the whole basin to fit it."

Zachary Thayne leaned forward on his wagon seat, gripping the reins so tightly that his knuckles stood out in shiny knobs. "You can't let this stop you, Doyle. Fargo killed my boy . . . there's no question in anybody's mind."

"Zachary," the sheriff said, "the judge can't issue a warrant on what folks think. There's got to be something stronger."

"He could've got rid of the gun," Zachary said. There was a wild look in his eyes. "You can't let Fargo go. . . ."

One of the tow-headed riders reined his horse against the wagon and grasped the old man's arm, stopping him. "Pa . . . this ain't doin' any good. Come away now . . . buryin' Peter's a-goin' to be hard enough as it is."

Zachary Thayne settled back in the seat. His hands were trembling. He sent Fargo a look of such malevolent hatred that it chilled Ives.

"This ain't done," Zachary said. "It ain't finished, Fargo."

He snapped the reins and the team hit their collars. The coffin rattled as the wagon pulled away. For a moment the girl continued to look back. Ives realized she was looking at him. Her eyes were the color of smoke—and filled with the same bitter hate. Then she turned away, and Ives was left with a distinct feeling of unreality.

Some of the townsmen were mounting horses along the street and falling in behind the wagon. The funeral procession reached the unpainted church at the end of the street and the line stopped while a parson in a celluloid collar climbed aboard the wagon. The procession started up again, heading toward the graveyard on the rise west of town.

Ives became aware that Sheriff Doyle was watching him. Without speaking, Ives thumbed one of his saddle-gun shells from a belt loop and held it out. It was a Henry .44. It matched neither of the shells in Doyle's hand. Doyle made no motion to take it. He was still studying Ives's face.

Ives hadn't shaved in a week and the roan-colored stubble of his beard had a greasy shine in the bright light. Dirty yellow weather stains mottled his ancient half-length sheepskin and there wasn't a button left on it. He was almost six feet tall, but exhaustion put a deep stoop in his shoulders and gave him a loose, sway-backed stance.

"All right, stranger," Doyle said. He tossed Cliff Fargo's shell back to him and replaced the bottleneck cartridge in his pocket. "I guess that closes the books for today," he said. "Going to the funeral, Jeff?"

"I aim to," the editor answered.

But he did not move to join Doyle as the sheriff started up the street. He seemed to hesitate by his door, studying Ives. It disturbed Ives.

"I'd still like that job," Ives said.

"You won't get it," Fargo said.

Russell sighed and shook his massive white head.

"Hold on, Cliff. We're gonna be short-handed as it is. I'd just as soon have a stranger. He won't have the stink of this trouble on him."

Fargo squinted suspiciously at Ives. "Where you from?"

"Rock Springs."

"You rode a hundred miles of desert just to get a job?"

"There wasn't anything in Rock Springs."

"I don't believe it," Fargo said.

Ives felt himself go stiff. He was exhausted from the long trip and he hadn't eaten in two days. It put his temper on a ragged edge and he wondered how much more of this man's poison he could take.

Russell motioned at the Appaloosa. It was a distinctly marked horse, a dark chest, almost blue, fading out to a white rump that was splashed with spots like a leopard's coat. "This your whole saddle string?" Russell asked.

"She's a good cutter," Ives said.

"She's a single-footer," Fargo said. "I never seen a single-footer yet that could cut worth a damn."

Ives wiped the back of his hand across his chapped lips. "Mister, why don't you go spit at the sheriff? I don't carry that bottleneck shell around in my pocket."

Fargo made an explosive sound. Russell grabbed his arm, checking what he might have done.

"This is my foreman," Russell told Ives. "If you work for me, you'll talk civil to him."

"I guess you've all got cause to be spooky," Ives said. "Why don't we back off and start over again?"

Fargo stared at Ives a moment longer, anger drawing his face so tight that it had a yellow shine across the cheek bones. Then he whirled and went to his roan. He swung aboard and spurred it into a gallop down the street.

"Cliff will cool down," Russell told Ives. "Fetch your horse and follow us out."

Russell turned to mount up, followed by the other hand who had stood with him. As they wheeled their horses away from the rack, Ives couldn't help glancing at Jeff Lee. The editor still stood in his doorway, stroking his long gray mustaches absently. He was looking at Ives's hands. They were strongly shaped hands. All the tiny lines of the skin had an etched look, as though some dark stain had been ground into it for a lifetime and could never be washed away.

"Son," Jeff Lee said, "are you sure you signed on with the right man?"

Ives looked at the shrewd, squinted eyes. He looked up at the sign above the door. He turned and crossed toward his mare and mounted her and headed her out of town. When he looked back, he saw that the editor was still in his doorway, watching.

II

The plank bridge trembled and gave off clattering echoes as Ives and the other three trotted across. The main road led eastward across the valley for ten miles to the Barricades. Ives had come in over those mountains and knew what an impregnable barrier they made between this basin and the outside world. It had taken him two days to get through the snow-choked Wind River Gap, and had almost finished his horse. The Anchor men left the main road at the forks just beyond the bridge, taking a wagon track southward into the long, tilted, wheat-grass meadows.

Fargo and Russell rode ahead, but the third man with them had dropped back to ride with Ives. He said his name was Hoback. Ives figured he must be near seventy. His long gray hair queued at the rear with a strip of rawhide, his deeply seamed cheeks, his lips, pursed and pleated against toothless gums, all gave his face an old-squaw look. He pulled a set of false teeth out of his shirt pocket and showed them to Ives.

"Vulcanite. No good. No damn' good at all. Make my gums so sore I can only wear 'em once a week, when I go to church. Damn Abilene dentist."

Ives glanced sharply at Hoback. He couldn't help it. The old man caught the look and squinted at Ives.

"Your name's familiar. Seems I heard it somewheres before. Or read it. You ever been in Abilene?"

"When were you in Abilene?" Ives asked carefully.

"I seen all them Kansas towns. Every year or so the boss sends some of us down to pick up some stockers. Last year it was Abilene . . . had to wait a few days for the cattle to come off the Chisholm. While I was there, I saw a hangin'. Ugly thing. Seems some cowhands had got drunk and shot up the town and a little girl was killed. This newspaper kept printing editorials about it . . . got the town in such a sweat that they went and strung up the cowhand they thought had killed the little girl. Come to find out later he was the wrong man."

Ives didn't say anything. Hoback looked at his hands. "You ever worked on a newspaper?" Hoback asked.

"I've worked at a lot of things," Ives said.

"Sure," the old man said. "That was a terrible thing about Lincoln, wasn't it?"

"What?" Ives asked.

"Abe Lincoln. This country'll miss him, Ives. They don't know how they'll miss him. I hope they catch this Booth feller and hang him from a hunnert-foot tree."

Ives frowned at Hoback, thinking at first that the man was mocking him. But Hoback was staring off into the distance with a sad look on his face and shaking his head gently from side to side. Ives thought Hoback must be getting senile. Abe Lincoln had been dead twenty years.

Ives didn't feel like talking any more. There was a bitter taste in his mouth. He thought about leaving. He wanted to leave. But he knew it was foolish. He was at the end of his rope. He had to bunk somewhere and eat somewhere. He couldn't go any farther. He had been stupid to think he could leave it behind. There would always be men like Hoback, remembering, asking questions, guessing the answers, or knowing them.

It was near evening when they reached the Anchor spread—a big hip-roof barn and a log house chinked with white alkali mud and a saddlebag bunkhouse and pack-pole corrals spreading out across the flats behind the buildings for half a mile. Russell said something to Fargo and angled away toward the house. The other three men continued to a pen next to the barn. Fargo dismounted and left his saddled horse tied to the fence, heading toward the bunkhouse. Hoback climbed off his flea-bitten mare, cursing an old man's stiff joints.

"Why don't you take your time off-saddling?" Hoback told Ives. "Happen you should stay down here till grub call, Fargo might be cooled off enough so's he won't stomp on your toes when you step in the bunk shack."

Ives was left alone with his Appaloosa. He was almost too exhausted to strip the horse, but she had been under saddle too long since Rock Springs, and he was afraid the rig was beginning to gall her. He had the cinch undone and was heaving the old-fashioned Mother Hubbard saddle off when a rider cantered around the barn.

It was a woman on a palomino, a horse the color of new gold, white-maned and white-tailed, one of the handsomest he'd ever seen. The woman rode side-saddle and wore a riding habit and Garibaldi blouse that would have been the height of fashion in any Eastern academy. A little porkpie hat of green velvet was almost lost in her wealth of dark hair, blown wild by the wind. She pulled the horse to a stop beside him and he could see that she had a fragile, sensitive face, flushed from the ride.

"Did you sign on for roundup?" she asked.

"Yes, ma'am. Name of Frank Ives."

"I'm Audrey Russell," she said. "Did Dad . . . I mean, did you come from town?"

"You mean about your foreman?" he said. "It seems the newspaper editor stretched things a bit. No warrant had been issued for Fargo. It looks like things are cleared up for him."

She touched her throat, giving a relieved sigh. "I'm so glad. I

Les Savage, Jr.

knew Cliff didn't do it. Dad wouldn't let me go. He was afraid of trouble."

"With that tow-headed outfit in the mountain wagon?"

"The Thaynes," she said.

"It was Peter Thayne who was killed?" Ives asked.

"That's right. Zachary Thayne's son . . . they found his body yesterday. . . ."

"I just hit the basin," he said. "Why should they blame your foreman for the killing? Why should the whole town jump to that conclusion?"

"It's the whole thing," she said. "The railroad trouble." She saw his blank face and gave an impatient shake of her head. She held out her hand and he took it, helping her dismount. She glanced up toward the house, then continued reluctantly. "Well . . . for so long Dad has been trying to get a railroad in here."

"Rock Springs is your nearest shipping point?" he said.

"That's right."

"A hundred-mile drive and most of it badlands," he said. "I came across that desert. Seventy, eighty miles without much water, and no graze. It must be a good trick to get a herd through."

"In dry years it's murder. Even in a good year we have to push them too fast to make it. Dad figures it melts off twenty or thirty pounds a head."

"At ten cents a pound. That's three dollars a head. If you drive a thousand that's a big loss."

"It's been the difference between winning or losing, these last years," she said. "If the price goes down a few cents, we're in the red."

"Where does the trouble come in? Somebody's fighting the railroad?"

"The Thaynes, Jeff Lee, practically the whole town. They

don't want Medicine Lodge turned into another trail town."

"It looks like a nice town," he said. "I guess a change wouldn't bother you much, living out here."

"I hadn't thought of it that way," she said.

"Have you ever seen a trail town?" he asked.

"No." She looked at him closely. "Have you?" she asked. He nodded slowly. She moistened her lips, saying softly: "Was it that bad?"

"Not like your town, Miss Russell," he said. "Not like any town you've ever seen, I guess."

She looked at him darkly. Then she gave the impatient shake of her head. "Let's drop it. We've been brooding too long around here. I want to forget the killing now, everything." She made an attempt to smile. It made her look younger, more a girl than a woman. A mischievous sparkle came to her eyes. "I'm really the boss around here, you know, and I put the new hands through a frightfully grueling test before I hire them."

"Something like unsaddling your horse?" he asked.

"How did you know? That's always the very first trial."

"And then maybe currying and graining?"

"Exactly. I didn't know my tyranny had become so famous."

He laughed. It was the first time he had laughed in weeks. She joined in, taking her porkpie hat off and brushing her hair back in a free, high-spirited gesture. He untied the latigo and pulled it free of the palomino's cinch ring.

"A beautiful animal," he said. "I don't think I've ever seen such a pure color."

Audrey put her arm around the horse's neck, running her fingers through the flaxen mane. "I've had Golden since I was thirteen. When I first got her, I tried to keep her in my room with me. Dad wouldn't let me take Golden in the house, so I spent most of that summer sleeping in the stall with her."

She gave the horse an affectionate squeeze. Then he saw the

mood leave her and the melancholy look touched her face again, turning it older. She was staring up toward the bunkhouse. He turned to see Cliff Fargo standing by the bunkhouse door, looking at them. Fargo started walking toward them.

"Well, Ives," Audrey said. "Thank you."

She turned almost hurriedly and went toward the main house. Ives watched her go, a half smile still on his face, thinking how strange she was, how changeable. Even when she laughed, there was a shadow behind it. He wondered if it was a reflection of the whole basin. It was a troubled basin. He was feeling the pressure of it more and more. He was sorry he had come.

He heaved the saddle off the palomino and slung it on the top rail of the corral, along with the saddle blanket. Then he took up the reins to lead the horse to the barn. By that time Fargo had reached him. The foreman was smoothing the yellow horsehide gloves on his hands, and looking off toward Audrey, as she climbed the porch of the house and disappeared inside. He stopped in front of Ives and held out a hand for the reins.

"I'll take care of the horse," he said.

"I don't mind."

"Ives, are you dumb, or just plain ornery?"

Fargo was still holding out his hand and Ives smiled as he gave the reins to the man. "Maybe a touch of both, Fargo."

"Don't call me that!" Fargo's voice was vicious. "That's one thing you can get straight from the beginning, Ives. Don't ever call me Fargo again!"

Fargo gave a brutal tug on the reins that made the palomino jump, and turned and led it toward the barn. Ives watched him go for a moment. But he was too tired to question any more, or even care. He finished stripping his mare and turned her into the corral. He got his war sack and his saddle roll and his booted rifle and started for the bunkhouse.

III

It was a saddlebag bunkhouse, with the bunk room and the kitchen divided by a roofed-over dogtrot that was open at either end. Hoback showed Ives to an empty bunk and Ives dumped his war sack down and opened it to get the skinning knife he'd been shaving with. He took off his sheepskin and his hickory shirt and rolled up the sleeves of his long-handled underwear and went outside to the wash trough. On a shelf was a dirty towel and a coffee can of thick yellow home-made soap. It was probably nothing but lard and ashes and he thought it was going to burn his hide off before he got the beard shaved.

The cook banged on a wagon tire to announce grub call and the crew began to drift in from the outlying corrals. Ives missed the good-natured hoorawing and joking he had become used to in other crews. They were a quiet, edgy bunch, and showed as much suspicion of a stranger as Fargo had. There was a bronco breaker named Kendricks. He was a cocky, sway-backed kid in shotgun chaps who ran off at the mouth about how he'd spurred the guts out of that buckskin, and how he'd break a pick handle across that broomtail's snout if she ever tried to bite him again, and how there wasn't another bronco stomper in the basin who could have busted that jugheaded roan the first time up. Nobody seemed to be listening much.

There was a half-breed named Quill who didn't talk at all, and a man named Parson with a black spade beard, and a man named Dave Gannett in a calico vest, who kept grinning and humming to himself while he washed, and five others whose names Ives didn't get.

They called the cook Sowbelly. He had a knobby baldhead, yellow as jaundice, and jowls that hung down in loose, furred dewlaps. He was as cantankerous as most of his breed and seemed to delight in making a horrible clatter among his pots and pans.

"Sowbelly!" Kendricks bawled. "Bring in the sinkers."

"There ain't no sinkers," Sowbelly said. "And there ain't no pie, and ain't no light bread. I'm outta flour and I'm outta dried apples and I'm outta coffee. You'll be eatin' sowbelly and pooch without no bread till we git some more grub from town." The crew began to howl and the cook had to clang on the wagon tire till they quieted down. "And we won't git any grub from town," he said sourly, "because they ain't got their spring shipment from Rock Springs. That early thaw has plugged up the gap so tight the freighters can't git beyond Twenty Mile. It'll be another week before they git through."

"Thaw, hell," Dave Gannett said. "This is some more of Zachary Thayne's doings. Ten to one he's been keeping those freighters from coming through the gap so's he could starve us out."

Kendricks began slamming the table with his empty tin plate. "I bet Thayne's got plenty of flour. I say we ride out there and git it. I say we. . . ."

He broke off with his mouth still open, staring at the door. The others turned to look and the noise died out quickly. Ives saw that Fargo had come in from outside and stood framed against the twilight. He pulled off his yellow roping gloves and took off his Mormon hat and put the gloves in the hat and set it on the shelf by the door. He took his seat at the end of the bench beside Quill.

"Thayne hasn't got anything to do with this," Fargo said. "The freighters couldn't git through and the food ain't here, and that's that. Now, does anybody have a gripe?"

Nobody said anything. Sowbelly set the kettle of stewed tomatoes in the middle of the table and the men started helping themselves. The breadless pooch wasn't very filling to a man as empty as Ives. He had three helpings and still felt hungry.

When he was finished, he crossed to the bunk room and

unlaced his saddle roll and spread the pair of worn blankets on the tick in his bunk. He started to undress. He shrugged out of the rawhide galluses that held up his jeans, and let them flop against his legs. He started to unbutton his jeans. Then he cursed sleepily and crawled into the bunk with his pants and boots still on. He ached all over, he was so tired. The last thing he heard was a pair of hands coming in to play poker.

Ives dreamed about Abilene. He was in the office of the *Gazette*, setting type for the Monday ads when he heard the sound of horses and the crash of gunfire. He ran outside—the Corkscrew outfit, galloping down Texas Street—more than he remembered (thousands of them), bigger and bigger until their horses filled the sky, rearing above him, taller than the buildings. Jack Border. Every rider looked like Jack Border. With his gun out. Smoking. Lisa Farraday—running into the street. The crash of gunfire. Lisa falling. Ives ran out to the little girl and saw that she was dead and she got smaller and smaller until she lay cupped in his hand, and then he was back inside the office and he was composing his editorial. He knew the words were wrong because he was accusing Jack Border of being the killer and he hadn't done that, he hadn't actually said Border killed Lisa, but he couldn't stop himself—the people, all the people were there, with the red, angry faces, shouting at him that they had lynched Border and he knew that was wrong, too, because it hadn't happened till after the paper was on the streets, but their faces changed and they all became Judge Parker's face telling him: "They've lynched the wrong man. Ives, you've gotten the wrong man killed, you've killed the wrong man, you've killed, killed, killed. . . ."

Ives shouted and put his hands over his eyes and it stopped. It all went away. But the guns were still crashing. He knew it couldn't be the guns because he was in the bunk room; he could feel the scratchy straw tick beneath him and could hear the hollow thump of sock-footed men dropping out of their bunks. But the guns were still crashing.

"Get a light," a man said. "Where's that lantern?"

"Don't do that," another man said. Ives recognized Parson's voice. "We'll make a prime target getting out that door with a light behind us."

"Where's my moccasins?" Hoback shouted. "Somebody stole my moccasins."

The door was swung open and Ives saw a man plunge through, a dark shape silhouetted against the strange yellow glow outside. Ives got up and ran out, holding his pants up with one hand and trying to pull the galluses over his shoulders with the other. The glow came from the barn. Flames reached skyward in long red streaks and a billow of smoke was pouring from the half-open door. In the treacherous firelight Ives could see a pair of riders galloping through the corrals. Then he saw who was shooting.

Cliff Fargo was crouched on one knee, halfway between the bunkhouse and the barn. He had his Spencer, emptying the seven-shot repeater methodically at the two horsemen. A couple of the others who had gotten out before Ives started banging away with their short guns but they didn't do any good.

Then one of Fargo's shots hit home and Ives saw the trailing horse stumble and go down. The man pitched free and rolled. He got dazedly to his hands and knees, a vague shadow just beyond the circle of firelight. Fargo took a shot at him and missed. He cocked the gun again, but the hammer snapped on an empty chamber.

"Kendricks!" Fargo shouted. "Hoback! Somebody give me your gun!"

Hoback ran toward him with a six-gun. But the second rider had circled back to pick up the unhorsed man. Ives could see a brief flurry of movement as the man afoot swung up behind the rider, and then the horse wheeled and was gone in the night. Fargo stood with Hoback's six-gun in his hand, cursing bitterly.

Tom Russell came running down from the house, still trying to button his pants under the flapping tails of a nightshirt. "Get the stock out of the barn!" he called. "You men, try to save the barn . . . !"

Ives was already heading for the building. He plunged through the door. The inside was thick with smoke. The hay in the loft was blazing and the whole back wall was going up in flames. The horses were screaming and whinnying in their stalls and kicking their slats out. Ives was deafened by the roar of the fire and the frantic crashing of animals. He tore open the first gate and managed to get one of the wagon team out without being kicked in the head. He slapped it on the rump and it ran, squealing, for the open door. Other men were in the barn now, opening the stalls farther down. The stampede of animals went past Ives in a wild rush and he had to throw himself against a stall to keep from being trampled. A pair of shadowy figures passed him, following the horses.

"The back wall's going!" one of them yelled. "Get out, Ives!"

He was about to follow when he saw a vague shape on the other side of the aisle, running the wrong way. He thought it was one of the men who had lost his direction.

"The other way!" Ives shouted. "Come back, you're turned around!"

The figure kept stumbling toward the rear. Part of the roof fell in with a crash, igniting a pile of hay at the rear of the aisle. The fresh burst of flame shot an eerie flash of light through the billows of smoke. In its glare Ives saw that the figure plunging toward the rear was Audrey Russell. She had a blanket over her head and he could hear her coughing in the smoke.

Ives went after her, shouting again: "Audrey, come back here!

It's too late!"

There was a new crash of falling timbers from the rear, hidden by the sooty clouds of smoke. Ives heard a horse screaming back there. He had almost caught up with Audrey when a burning rafter collapsed above her. It fell across her shoulders and drove her to her knees. The blanket caught fire and Ives reached her and tore it off her head, kicking the blazing rafter aside. He took her under the arms and lifted her to her feet. She was crying in pain. There was a hysterical sound to her voice and she pounded at him and fought to get free.

"Golden!" she screamed. "I've got to get Golden!"

"You can't," he said. "We'll be lucky to get out ourselves."

He heard the shriek of yielding timbers and turned to see the whole back wall coming down at them through the smoke with a roaring crash. He lifted Audrey off her feet and lunged toward the front of the barn. He heard the wall strike just behind them. A portion of the roof followed. He felt the earth tremble beneath his feet and a shower of sparks drowned him. Charred shingles and lengths of wood rained from above. He was battered to his knees by a section of blazing rafter. He rose again, dragging Audrey with him. She was still fighting him hysterically.

"Golden!" she called. "Golden . . . !"

The smoke blinded him and made him cry. It choked him and burned his lungs and he could hardly keep from doubling over in a paroxysm of coughing. He heard shouting voices from the front of the barn and it guided him. Men came running out of the smoke and took his struggling burden from him and helped him out the door. He couldn't hear the horse screaming at the rear of the barn any more. All he could hear was the roar of collapsing walls.

They got him to a water trough and doused his smoldering clothes. Audrey was sitting down beside the trough with her hands over her face, crying. Tom Russell was on one knee beside her, trying to soothe her. The rest of the men had formed a bucket brigade and were trying to keep the fire from spreading.

Sowbelly came from the cook shack with a bucket of lard. Russell tried to rub some of it on Audrey's burns, but she pushed him off. She had gotten herself under control now and had stopped crying. Her face was pale, strained, glistening with tear streaks. She pulled her skirts around her and rose, carrying the bucket of lard over to Ives where he sat against the trough, spent from the struggle in the barn. She knelt beside him. Her voice trembled. "Thank you, Ives."

"I'm sorry we couldn't make it. I mean . . . Golden."

She closed her eyes. Her lips were drawn and compressed. Fargo came walking from among the corrals, Hoback's six-shooter still gripped in one fist.

"It was the Thaynes," he said. "That horse I shot has a Fiddleback brand."

Audrey opened her eyes and looked off into the night. There was a deep bitterness in her voice. "They thought we killed Peter Thayne. Maybe I wish we had."

Looking up at her, Ives didn't know what to say. She became aware of him watching her. She touched her face self-consciously, gave a savage little shake of her head.

"This isn't helping you any, is it?" she said. She fingered out some lard and started rubbing it on his burned face. "You tell me where."

"Feels like one on the forehead . . . a little higher."

Russell came from the fire line, irritably brushing soot from his tufted white brows. "Ives, I need a couple of men. You in shape to ride?"

"Wait, Dad," Audrey said. "At least until you can take the whole crew."

"I can't wait any longer. I've got to leave men here to control the fire, Audrey. The Thaynes can't go very far riding double.

Chances are they'll head straight for home . . . either to hole up or git another horse. Now fetch a gun, Ives. If your Appaloosa's too beat, rope yourself an Anchor horse."

Ives got slowly to his feet. He didn't want to get his gun. He didn't want to go after the Thaynes with a gun. It made him realize he should quit—now—before it was too late. He should have known the place was wrong for him when he first rode into Medicine Lodge and saw the dead man and the bitter clash in the street, and knew it was a troubled range. Such a thing was a bog that could pull a man down. He had his own battle to fight. He couldn't afford to get involved in anybody else's trouble.

Russell had been watching him narrowly and finally said: "You got Anchor's beans in your belly, Ives. I didn't mark you for a hand that would quit come the first rough crossing."

Ives looked at the man sharply. He knew Russell was right. He had pledged himself to the brand. He had done it by eating their food and sleeping in their bunkhouse, and now he owed them something. It was the code of the range. It made a bitter taste in his mouth and he couldn't help thinking how illogical loyalty was. But he'd made a deal. Logical or not, he'd be disgusted with himself if he backed out now.

He went to the bunkhouse and put his sheepskin on over his underwear. He buckled his gun belt around that and got his Henry in its scabbard and went back to the corrals. Hoback was roping out his horse. The farther north Ives got, the longer the ropes seemed to run. Hoback's dally must have been sixty feet. Ives borrowed the line when Hoback was finished and got his Appaloosa. Russell had offered him an Anchor horse, but Ives figured the Appaloosa had gotten enough rest, and he didn't feel up to learning a strange bronco's tricks in the middle of the night.

IV

The barn was still burning, casting its eerie glow over the black fretwork of corrals, when the five men rode out of Anchor. Tom Russell rode in the lead with Fargo. Behind them trailed the young bronco stomper, with Ives and Hoback bringing up the rear.

It was too dark to look for signs. They took the wagon track through the miles of tilted meadowland till they reached the river road and turned on the road toward the Barricades. The earth was still wet from recent rain and the horses plowed up the sod and raised a sweet rich smell that was a million years old. None of the men talked and the only sound was the creak of saddles and the hollow wheeze of horses. Ives kept wondering what Russell planned to do. He couldn't believe the man meant to raid or burn in retaliation. Such a blind revenge didn't fit in with the picture Ives had formed of Russell. Ives wouldn't have come if he thought this was what the man intended.

After a long while a wind rose against them, carrying a new smell, the perfume of a damp pine forest. Ives could sense the black mass of the mountains ahead of them and the horses began to work harder against the rising land.

"The gap ain't far," Hoback said.

"Thayne country?" Ives asked.

"The center of it," Hoback said. "Zachary Thayne acts like the whole basin's really his'n. He was the first white man to come through the gap. He fought the Indians for the basin before they even heard of Custer. Homestead Act, Pre-emption Act, Timber Culture Act . . . he took land under all of 'em. Thayne land straddles about half the gap. There ain't any other way the railroad can get into the basin from the east."

"And Thayne isn't selling out."

"He says it was him and his brother that founded the town

and they ain't seeing it turned into a hell hole like the other railheads."

"Couldn't the railroad condemn enough for a right of way?"

"If they wanted to they could. But the Thaynes started shooting the minute them Wyoming Central surveyors showed on their land. It spooked the railroad. They don't want another Royal Gorge war. They ain't too convinced they could make money on this trunk line anyway. It's Tom Russell that pushed 'em into the idea. . . ." Hoback trailed off. Then he made a whimpering little sound, and said: "Ives, don't go in there. They've drove us clear back to Cemetery Ridge and Longstreet's a-coming with his whole corps. All they got to do is get one Reb batt'ry on Little Round Top and we won't. . . ."

"Hoback," Ives said softly.

"What?" Hoback said. He was silent for a moment, and then his saddle creaked. He let out his breath in a long sigh. "You got to make allowances, Ives. I'm an old man. Sometimes my mind wanders. Was I talking about Manassas?"

"You were talking about Gettysburg."

"Ah. You know something? I guess I was an old man even then."

The mountains closed in. The road was pinched against the river and they rode through aspens, black at the base, startlingly white higher up, like shafts of moonlight in the darkness. Ives could feel no wind but the trees made a constant quaking rustle all about him.

He had ridden through Wind River Gap when he entered the basin and knew what a narrow trough it made, knew how the rock walls towered above the road, so close together at the top that sometimes the strip of sky seemed no broader than a rifle barrel. And he had seen the snow. The big spring thaws hadn't come yet, but the sun was melting snow on the heights and sending slides down that choked the gap from one end to the other. It was what was holding the freight wagons up at Twenty Mile, the way station at the other end of the gap. The freighters had even warned Ives not to try it. But his string had been almost played out and a starving man couldn't afford to wait.

With Russell leading, the Anchor crew reached the first drift. It covered the gap from wall to wall and the men had to drive their horses through it belly-deep. A hundred yards beyond it they reached another slide and had to skirt it by swimming their animals in the icy river.

They moved on, fighting the snow all the way, till they finally reached a break in the south wall of the cañon. A side road left the main gap and turned into the transverse gorge, shelving up its rocky walls to the timberland above Wind River Gap. The faint light of dawn was beginning to seep through the fir forest and the jays were coming awake and cawing at the riders. Russell turned and said something to Fargo. The foreman angled away, disappearing in the dark timber. The others rode for another hundred yards to the edge of a park.

On the far side of the broad meadow Ives could see the outfit, a shapeless sprawl of buildings and corrals in the eerie gray light. As the men rode into the open, hounds began to bay from the house. The riders were halfway across the meadow when the front door was opened and the pack of dogs rushed out. There were half a dozen of them, flooding across the meadow. They surrounded the horses. The rock faces of nearby slopes echoed to the baying until the meadow seemed drowned in the wild sound. The hounds snapped at the horses and leaped against the riders. Ives's mare squealed and kicked at her tormentors. Russell's horse reared high and the man tore off his hat, whipping it down at the dogs.

"Zachary!" he shouted. "It's Tom Russell! Call off your damned hounds!"

"Don't try to come in, Russell!" a man called from the house.

"Get out of here! We don't have no business with you!"

One of the hounds was trying to hamstring Kendricks's bay and the horse almost pitched the young bronco rider. Kendricks cursed viciously, fighting the panicked horse, and pulled his six-gun. The first shot blasted echoes against the mountains that came back multiplied to the crashing of a dozen guns. A dog leaping up at Kendricks jerked in mid-air and fell back to the ground in a heap. Kendricks went on firing, cursing every time he shot.

"Kendricks!" Ives shouted. "Stop it! You don't have to do that. . . ."

His voice was drowned by the crash of gunfire echoing insanely back and forth across the meadow. While Kendricks was still shooting, Ives saw the door of the house open wide. The dim figure of a man lunged out, a rifle in his hands. By that time Kendricks had emptied his gun. Four dogs lay sprawled on the ground and the other two had been frightened back by the deafening gunfire. They circled wide, their baying turned to weird howls. As the shattering echoes of gunfire died away, the man at the cabin shouted in rage.

"Damn you, Russell!"

Ives saw the rifle come up and thought the man was going to fire. But a sound from within the cabin halted him, a girl's voice, shrill and startled.

"Pa . . . Pa!"

Russell called to the man at the door. "Put up your gun, Zachary! We've got you whipsawed! Fargo's in the cabin behind you now!"

Zachary Thayne hesitated, then turned and took a step back to the door to see inside. Russell spurred his horse confidently toward the cabin. Ives hesitated, looking at the dogs on the ground, sickened by what had happened.

"Kendricks," he said, "you must feel brave as hell."

The bronco buster stiffened in the saddle, starting to say something. But Ives didn't wait to hear. He swung off his horse and walked among the dogs, bending to inspect each one. Three were dead. The other was moving feebly and whining. His chest had been shattered. Hoback moved his horse over beside Ives and looked at the hound.

"You won't save that one," the old man said.

"He's suffering," Ives said.

"You do it, Ives. I can't do it."

Ives got his Henry from the saddle scabbard, levering a shell into the chamber. He stood over the dog a moment. Then he forced himself to put the rifle muzzle against the animal's head and pulled the trigger.

Kendricks had already gone after Russell and the two of them were dismounting by the door. They were inside by the time Ives and Hoback reached the cabin. Somebody had lighted a lamp inside and through the open door Ives saw the girl first. The blonde girl he had seen in the wagon in town.

She stood near a rickety plank table. She was barefoot and had a wrapper clutched about her slender body. She looked to be nineteen or so, the same elfin face Ives had seen in town, making him think of a river witch, untamed, uncaught. He couldn't define its haunting quality. Maybe the lips were too full, or too red. It made them look pouting, child-like. But there was nothing child-like about the eyes. They were a woman's eyes, exotically tilted, heavy-lidded with hate for Anchor. Shadows seemed to come and go in some secret game beneath the Slavic slant of her fragile cheek bones. Her hair had a corn-tassel shimmer, hanging in thick blonde coils about her shoulders. Ives wondered if it had ever seen a comb.

Zachary Thayne stood protectively beside her, still holding his buffalo gun. He was barefoot, and the tails of a homespun nightshirt dangled outside hastily donned britches. His lips were bloodless and blue with outrage in the hoary gray tangle of his beard.

Beyond the man and girl Ives could see Fargo, standing just within the half-opened back door. Ives realized it must have been simple to surprise the girl while the dogs were diverted by the riders coming in from the front. Fargo held a six-shooter in one hand. He must have lighted the Betty lamp himself. It sat on the chair beside him, shaped like a covered gravy dish and burning camphene that filled the room with a smell of turpentine and alcohol.

"Zachary," Russell said, "one of your horses is lyin' dead fifty feet from my barn. It's clear proof you was there."

"It doesn't prove a thing," Zachary said. He had a rumbling voice, resonant as a bass drum. "You could have picked the horse up on open range and took him there and shot him."

Russell was beginning to turn red. "A dozen of my hands saw two of your riders. Now either you produce your sons or we'll take you and Sabina in for the burning."

"Why not just take me?" the girl said. Her voice was soft and trembling with anger. "You could shoot me like you did Peter, or maybe hang me along the road to town. . . ."

"Sabina," Zachary said sharply. It stopped her, and Zachary looked at the cattleman. "All right, Russell. If you've a mind to . . . take us in."

Russell's scowl drew his shaggy white brows so low they almost hid his eyes. "You mean it was you . . . you're admitting it was you?"

"I'm admitting nothing. We'll let the court decide that."

Russell hesitated, then turned to Ives and Hoback, still standing outside. "Git a couple of their horses from the barn," Russell said.

Zachary glanced quickly at Hoback. "There are horses in that pen behind the house."

Hoback started to go around back, but Fargo said sharply: "Wait a minute. He's too anxious to git us away from here. What's in that barn, Zachary?"

"Nothing," Zachary said. "If they was there, don't you think they'd be gone by now?"

"Hoback would've seen 'em," Fargo said. "We was pretty close behind 'em and we must've caught up some, with them riding double. I wonder if we didn't come in here right on their heels." Fargo waved his six-shooter. "Put that buffalo gun down, Zachary. You and me are going to have a look-see."

Zachary looked at Fargo's gun a long time before he finally laid the .50-caliber Sharps on the table. Fargo moved in behind him and jabbed him in the kidneys with the gun. Ives backed away from the door to let them through. Fargo started toward the barn, driving Zachary before him. Russell told Hoback to stay at the cabin with the horses, and to keep Sabina there.

Russell and Kendricks and Ives followed Fargo at a distance of ten feet. Their boots made a muffled crunch in the thick bed of pine needles. The two remaining dogs circled Fargo, whining, panting, looking expectantly at Zachary. The morning sun was beginning to flood the meadow with a glowing yellow light. A woodpecker started drumming far back in timber. Fifteen feet from the barn Fargo stopped Zachary.

"Orin!" he called. "Eric! I've got your pa out here with a gun in his back. You start any shooting and you'll be killing him. Now come out with your hands up."

There was no answer. The sun was drawing a gray steam out of the damp ground and filling the air with the scent of pine and pitch. A whiskey jack scolded from a nearby tree.

Fargo jabbed Zachary and they walked forward again. Ives kept a hand on his holstered Colt. Fargo reached the door. It was open a crack and he put a boot against it and gave a shove. It opened with a creak. Fargo stood with his gun in Zachary's back and Ives saw a mirthless grin touch his mouth. Ives moved in behind with the others, and, when his eyes had adjusted to the gloom within the barn, Ives could see what made Fargo smile.

Near the rear of the barn, beside a saddled horse streaked with drying lather, stood the two tow-headed men Ives had seen riding into town with the dead body yesterday. One of them still held a six-gun gripped in his fist, aimed at the door.

"Drop it, Orin," Fargo said.

Orin made a soft, ugly sound and let the gun slip from his hand. He was a lean young man, almost as narrow in the shoulders as he was in the hips. He had a bony face, all hollows and angles, and his blue eyes looked red-rimmed and feverish. Ives thought he'd never seen a boy so jumpy-looking. If he'd been a horse, a man wouldn't go near him for fear of being kicked.

His brother Eric was a younger edition of Zachary—the same wild tangle of hair, the same rocky features. His Levi's and blue serge vest were streaked with drying yellow lather off the horse.

"What happened?" Fargo asked Zachary. The old man didn't answer and Fargo jabbed him hard with the gun. "You knew they were in here."

Zachary's shoulders sagged. "I heard them come in. They didn't even have time to leave the barn before you showed up."

"They'll be leaving now," Russell said. "Eric, saddle yourself a horse."

"You might as well let me saddle one, too," Zachary said. "I'm going with you."

Eric looked stolidly at Russell for a moment. It was hard for Ives to guess what he was thinking. He didn't show Orin's feverish anger. Finally, moving deliberately, Eric lifted a one-ear bridle off a peg on the wall and went to get a roan out of a rear stall.

Fargo looked at Orin and jerked his gun at the horse they had ridden double. "You can take that one, Orin. Bring him outside. Kendricks, tell Hoback to bring our horses down here."

Kendricks walked to the door and looked toward the house. "Hoback's already coming," he said. "The girl's with him."

Orin had picked up the trailing reins of the saddled animal. Fargo jerked his gun toward the door and Orin led the horse out. Fargo trailed him, with Russell and Ives bringing up the rear. Fargo hung back a little so he could keep an eye on the other two Thaynes. Russell and Ives stopped just outside the door. Ives saw Hoback leading three of the horses from the house. The girl was on his flank with the other two. When he was within twenty feet of the barn, Hoback called sheepishly: "She had to come down here. No use arguing with a buzz saw."

Orin had led his horse outside till he was about ten feet from the barn, and Fargo called sharply: "That's far enough, Orin!"

Ives saw that Sabina was beginning to drop back, letting Hoback get ahead of her. There was something furtive about it, stirring suspicion in Ives. Before he could say anything, Sabina dropped the reins of one horse and used the other reins to lash Hoback's horses across the rump. They squealed and reared and tried to lunge free. For an instant Hoback held them, but the girl continued to shout and lash them wildly and it drove them frantic. Hoback was thrown aside by one of the plunging animals, losing the reins, and they bolted at a dead run, directly toward the barn door.

It all happened so fast that the men at the barn had little time for reaction. Orin was the only one far enough out to escape by getting away from the barn. He managed to pull his horse out of the way as the four animals stampeded past him. Ives started to dodge aside against the wall, but saw he would be too late, and turned to run into the barn.

Fargo was standing inside and Ives saw him wheel and plunge

into the safety of an open stall. Russell was running just ahead of Ives. He tried to change direction and get out of the way. It tripped him up. Ives saw him start to go down directly in the path of the horses. Ives threw himself at Russell, knocking the man aside as he fell. The first thundering horse brushed past them. They hit rolling and were out of the way, sprawled in the hay to the right of the door, when the following horses charged past.

The animals stampeded on down the aisle, past the stalls where Eric and Zachary were saddling up. The horses saw the back wall and tried to stop themselves, rearing and wheeling. But they couldn't pull up soon enough. The whole barn shuddered as they crashed against the wall and the place was a bedlam of whinnying and screaming. Mingled with all the noise inside Ives could hear Sabina's voice.

"Orin . . . now, now!"

Ives saw Fargo lunging for the door. Ives rose and followed the man, getting there an instant after Fargo. Outside, Orin had mounted the horse he was holding. He raked it with his spurs and it started in a dead run for the timber. Fargo cursed and raised his gun. Orin was still only fifteen feet away and Fargo was aiming squarely at the middle of his back.

Ives shouted, knocking the gun up. It went off at the sky, and, before Fargo could recover, Ives tore the gun from his hand and threw it as far as he could. Then he ran for the horse Sabina had held.

It was the Quarter horse Russell had ridden and the excitement had made it spook about ten feet from Sabina, but the dragging reins had ground-hitched it there. When she saw what Ives intended, Sabina ran for the horse, too. She shouted and waved her arms, trying to scare it into a run. The horse started shying and backing off, but Ives caught up with the girl before she could do any more damage. He grabbed her by the arm and swung her aside so hard that she almost fell. The skittish horse was still backing away and it took Ives two more lunging steps to get the reins.

He swung aboard and went after Orin. The man had disappeared in the timber behind the cabin, apparently heading for a cañon that broke the ridge overlooking the park. Ives knew that Orin's horse was spent from the hard ride carrying double, and spurred his animal into a dead run through the trees. In a few moments he caught up with Orin. He saw him ahead, a shadowy shape in the timber, his horse already beginning to falter and stumble as it ran. The Quarter horse was bred for a short run and it was what beat Orin. Ives caught up with the man just as he felt the first burst of speed begin to fade in the Quarter horse.

He brought the animal in beside Orin's laboring horse and threw himself out of the saddle at the man. For a moment they both hung on Orin's horse as Orin fought to stay in the saddle. Then they pitched off. The thick mat of pine needles broke their fall and threw them apart.

They got to their feet about the same time. Orin lunged at Ives with a savage curse. Ives ducked under Orin's first blow and threw himself across the man's legs. It knocked Orin down again with Ives beside him on his knees. Before Orin could recover, Ives grabbed his arm and flopped him over on his belly. He twisted the arm into a hammer lock, driving Orin's face into the mat of needles.

"Now, slack off, damn you," Ives panted. "I'm trying to keep you from getting killed."

Orin struggled feebly. Ives twisted his arm higher. Orin gave up, and Ives let him get his face out of the pine needles. The sound of horses crashing through the timber came to them and in a moment Fargo rode up. Ives didn't think he'd ever seen anybody so mad. Fargo's face was livid and for a moment he couldn't even speak. Tom Russell came in behind, riding Hoback's horse. Fargo finally found his voice.

"You and me, Ives," he said. "The next time, just you and me."

Tom Russell pulled to a halt and sat, drooped in the saddle, breathing heavily. "No, Cliff," he said. "Ives was right. A burned barn ain't worth a killin'. I know you wouldn't've done it, anyway. You ain't the kind to shoot a man in the back."

Fargo glanced at Russell sharply. Ives had expected anger, but there wasn't any. It was gone suddenly from Fargo's face, replaced by an expression Ives could hardly define. Fargo's lips were parted, though he didn't say anything. It made him look young, strangely vulnerable. For a moment it was completely silent, and Ives tried to read what was happening between the two men. Then Fargo reined his horse around, hard. Faced away from Ives, without looking at him, Fargo said: "All right. Let's git him to town. Let's git this over with."

V

At dawn that morning Jefferson Lee was setting type. The *Clarion*'s office was divided by a wooden rail across the middle and the editor stood in the rear section, his back to the ancient Albion hand press. He worked without his shirt and his long-handled underwear was gray from long use, bagged at the elbows, and frayed sadly around the neck. He had dropped his braces from his shoulders so that they hung in loops against the back of his legs, allowing his pants to sag down around his gaunt hips.

The type case sat on the sloping frames before him and he was slipping the oily ten-point type from the case into his type stick. He worked slowly because the case was almost empty and he hated to think of moving another one onto the frames. Doc Cabell had warned him to stop the heavy work. He could feel the pains in his chest every time he had to lift a case or shift a galley. But how in the hell did they expect a man to get out his newspaper?

He had been without a type slinger for six weeks now. Compositors were a traveling bunch, always drifting, but Jeff had a suspicion that the last one had been scared off by Tom Russell. Jeff grinned sardonically, wondering if Russell had really thought that would stop the *Clarion*'s tirades against Anchor.

The type stick was full and he justified the line and turned to set it in the galley. He sighed, absently combing his fingers through his mustaches. Then he cursed, pulling his fingers away and looking at their ink-stained tips.

A rattle at the door startled him. He crossed the room, pushing through the gate in the dividing rail. He halted a moment at the desk, glancing at the enormous cap-and-ball revolver he kept in one of the pigeonholes. He had used it in the Civil War and had never gotten it converted to handle cartridges. Peter Thayne's death had made him jumpy, and last night for the first time in years he had loaded the gun.

He gave a crotchety shake of his head, and moved on to the door without the six-shooter. The shades were drawn and he pulled one aside a crack to see who stood outside. The man was dimly visible in the pale dawn, a stranger, definitely not Anchor. Jeff unlocked the door and opened it.

"I saw your light," the man said. "I'd like some information."

Jeff backed into the office and the man followed. The Argand lamp was still glowing on the desk at the rear and its light gave Jeff a clearer picture of the man. He had his hands in the pockets of a yellow-stained sheepskin and his lye-colored pants were caked with mud to the knees. His eyes were heavy-lidded like those of a man fighting sleep and his mouth was slack with exhaustion. His gaunt face was brick-red, burned so badly by the sun that it was scaling. A week's beard made its greasy blond stubble on his jaw.

"You newspapermen are all alike," he said.

"Like cats, we do our best thinking after midnight," Jeff said. "You want a subscription?"

He saw that the man was carefully searching the back section of the office as they talked. He took one hand out of his sheepskin pocket and scratched irritably at the blond stubble on his jaw.

"Nobody else work with you?"

"I sent an ad to the Rock Springs *Sentinel* six weeks ago for a type slinger," Jeff said. He looked at the man's hand. "You ain't him."

"No. But I'm looking for a man of that stripe. He was headed up this way from Rock Springs. If he got a job anywhere, it might be on a newspaper."

"A friend of yours?"

"Frank Ives was his name. A man near thirty, yellow sheepskin somethin' like mine, riding an Appaloosa mare."

Jeff tried to mask any reaction, but something must have showed in his face, some small change that caught the other man's attention. He leaned toward Jeff.

"You've seen him."

"No. But if I do, I'll tell him you're looking for him. What name should I give him?"

The man looked at the printing press behind Jeff. He said: "Never mind. He'll know me when he sees me."

He turned around and tramped out. Jeff followed to close the door after him. He saw the man mount a claybank and head down the street. The horse was matted with mud and had apparently thrown a shoe, because it limped on the off-hind leg. Jeff watched until the rider stopped before the Ephron Livery Stables a block down the street. The man dismounted and banged on the barn, sending clapping echoes throughout the town, until George Ephron appeared. The stranger apparently made a deal with George to stable the horse, and then crossed to disappear in the hotel.

Jeff went thoughtfully back to his work. The stranger only whetted his interest in Ives. He had been intrigued with Ives when he first saw him. He had seen the ink stains on Ives's hands. A newspaperman who didn't want to work at his trade.

When he had finished setting the type and blocking it into a proof form, Jeff knocked off for breakfast at the hotel. He learned that the stranger had gone directly up to his room, but it was a slipshod, one-horse hotel and the clerk rarely bothered to get any names in the register. It was after 9:00 when Jeff returned to his office. He rolled the galley proof and was starting to correct it when he heard the cavalcade coming down the street outside. He had run up his shades, and through the windows he could see all four of the Thaynes coming down the street, with five Anchor men flanking them. Fargo and Tom Russell both had their saddle guns out, held across their pommels, and their faces looked grim.

Sensing fodder for his Wednesday edition, Jeff hurried outside. The sheriff's office and jail was half a block down the street, a narrow adobe building jammed between Ephron's big hip-roofed barn and the saloon. Sheriff Doyle must have seen the riders coming. As they pulled up to his rack, Doyle stepped out of the door. When he was on official business, Doyle always wore his hard hat and a sawed-off .32 Smith & Wesson with a stud trigger stuck through his belt. As Jeff approached the crowd, he heard Tom Russell speak.

"I want a warrant sworn out, Doyle. Eric and Orin. They burned my barn last night and half a dozen horses were killed."

Doyle looked at the Thaynes, but none of them said anything. Doyle tilted his hat back with a thumb and said: "Well, Tom, we'll have to do it right. You come in and swear out the complaint. I'll take it to the judge and see if he'll issue a warrant." He glanced at Orin and Eric. "Step down, boys. You're in custody."

Orin and Eric grudgingly dismounted, along with Tom Russell, and they all went inside with Doyle. Zachary and Sabina got off their horses and were about to follow when they were stopped by the sight of Zachary's brother coming across the street from his general store. Silas Thayne was the antithesis of Zachary—a placid, round-faced, balding little man. He probably hadn't changed his shirt in two weeks, but every morning he put on a fresh, starched white dickey to cover its soiled front. It always reminded Jeff of the smug propriety with which a town covered its sins.

Curtly Zachary told his brother what had occurred, and Silas waggled his head. "I told you what would happen if you let those young hotheads out of your sight, Zachary."

Zachary made a disgusted sound. "Why don't you go bunk with Anchor?"

"Now, now," Silas said mildly. "There's no cause to contend again. Just because a man tries to keep an open mind." He broke off as Zachary snorted and turned to go inside. Silas caught his arm, checking him. "If Doyle holds the boys . . . I mean, there's no use in you riding back to the gap. You and Sabina can use the extra room till this thing is settled. And if there's any need for bail, you know I'll be glad to loan. . . ."

"We don't want no money that has an Anchor stink," Zachary said. He pulled free to go inside. Silas followed, shaking his head. More townsmen were gathering, and by now most of the Anchor crew were off their horses, stretching their legs and answering questions. Jeff had seen Frank Ives among them. The editor moved over to Ives and said in a low voice: "Man here looking for you. Big, built like a Conestoga horse, hemp-colored hair, forked a claybank with a Corkscrew brand."

Jeff saw emotion shuttle over Ives's face, fear, apprehension, bitterness, he couldn't tell which. Finally Ives looked toward the south, and his shoulders sagged. In a barely audible voice he said: "Border."

"He didn't tell me his name," Jeff said.

"Tom Border," Ives said. He was staring emptily into some vast distance and Jeff felt he was talking to himself.

"Well," Jeff murmured, "he's at the hotel now. I figure he'll be sleeping through the next ten or twelve hours. He looked even more beat out than you." Jeff paused, then smiled at Ives. "They won't be finished here for some time. How about a cup of coffee?"

Ives looked across the street at the *Clarion* office. His eyes drew almost shut and he rubbed his hand tiredly over his face. Jeff saw the reluctance in him.

"No obligation, Ives," he said softly.

Something seemed to let go in Ives. His shoulders drooped and he let out a long tired breath. He turned with Jeff and they crossed to the newspaper office. In the rear of the building, behind the press, Jeff had his living quarters—a cot that was never made, a soapstone stove, and a set of shelves for his food and dishes. There was always a pot of coffee on and all he had to do was stoke up the fire. Ives sank into the leather armchair next to the bed. He looked for a moment at the Albion press.

"Meet Horace Greeley," Jeff said. "Best hand press west of the Mississippi. Horace can still run an issue faster than those damn' treadle presses they got in the big towns."

Ives didn't say anything. He leaned his head back and closed his eyes.

"This Tom Border," Jeff said. "Is he gunning for you?"

Ives didn't open his eyes. "I guess that's it."

Studying the young man, Jeff idly started combing his mustaches. Then he glanced down and saw that his fingers were still ink-stained.

"Dammit," he said. "I'll either have to give up setting type or shave off this soup strainer." He crossed to the press and got a rag, wiping his hands clean and futilely trying to rub the stain off his mustaches. He looked at Ives's hands. He said musingly: "I had a feeling you were running from something when I first saw you, Ives. Is it really from Tom Border? Or is it from yourself?"

Ives didn't answer. The coffee was boiling and Jeff poured two cups, taking one to Ives. Ives held the cup in his hand, staring at it, and finally he began talking. His voice was low and strained and full of hopelessness, like a man who had kept something bottled up inside him for too long, and had to talk to somebody.

"Abilene was the hot end of hell, Lee, particularly after Wild Bill Hickock left. This Corkscrew was a big outfit, up from Texas every year with a big trail herd to ship. They were hell-raisers, with a boss that set them a prime example. He was Jack Border, Tom Border's brother. One Sunday morning the whole crew got drunk and started shooting up the town just about the time church let out. An eight-year-old girl named Lisa Farraday was killed. A coroner's jury was called, and, while it was in session, I got out a special edition. My editorial heated the town up so much that a lynch mob marched out to the Corkscrew camp and strung up Jack Border. While they were doing it, an eyewitness was appearing before the coroner's jury, swearing that Border's gun couldn't have done the killing. Jack Border was half a block down the street, firing into the air, when Lisa was hit."

"Could this have been a Corkscrew witness?" Jeff asked.

"No, it was somebody who couldn't be bought, a responsible man who must have been telling the truth. He named the actual killer, a drunk Corkscrew hand who hasn't been found yet, as far as I know."

"In your editorials, did you actually accuse Jack Border of the killing?"

"No, it was just a general thing, a tirade against what Border stood for, against conditions that would allow such a thing to occur. You've probably written a hundred of them."

"And you blame yourself for Jack Border's death?"

"It was what touched off the mob. Words. I used to talk about their power before. I never really knew. They're more dangerous than a gun."

Jeff looked at Ives's hands. "It takes a long time to wash that ink stain out of your hide, Ives. I don't think you ever get it out of your blood."

"Not even when it's been burned out?"

"I can understand Jack Border's being on your conscience, Ives. But right or wrong, you'll come back to this business. You're no cattleman. How long do you think you can fool Anchor?"

"I can do their work. I was born and raised on a cattle ranch. Texas. But it didn't satisfy me. When I was eighteen, I went on the bum. I learned typesetting in Dallas. I guess I got my fingers dirty on every press between there and the Mississippi."

Jeff smiled. It was an old story, his own story, farther East. His father had owned a dry-goods store and the smell of new flannel still made him want to leave town.

"I lost my type slinger about six weeks ago," Jeff said. "I've got a bum ticker and the work's something of a load. The job's open . . . if you want it."

Ives looked at the press. He rose and crossed the room and put his empty coffee cup on the table. He stood with his back to Jeff.

"You wouldn't have anything to do with the writing," Lee said.

"I'd be part of it," Ives said. "What have you got here? One man's already dead. Who's right? Who's wrong? Is it criminal to want a railroad in this valley?"

"The misuse of power is criminal. That's what I've attacked Tom Russell for, from the beginning. A man's got to write the truth as he sees it."

"How does he know it's the truth? The Thaynes don't exactly wear halos. Will you tell how they tried to burn Anchor out?"

"I'll also tell why they did it."

"Peter Thayne was shot out on the range. Nobody saw it and nobody proved Russell had anything to do with it."

"You're fighting windmills, Ives. There's a bigger question. Do you really think Tom Russell has the right to turn this town into another Abilene?"

Ives stared at him without answering. The young man's face looked haggard and pale and unutterably weary. His eyes were bloodshot and red-rimmed from lack of sleep and the grooves were cut deeply on either side of his mouth. Jeff thought he had never seen a man who needed to stop and rest so badly.

Finally Ives said: "Thanks for the coffee. They're probably finished over there by now."

Jeff walked out onto the street with him. Some of the crowd was still gathered around the sheriff's office. Zachary and his daughter were walking with Silas Thayne toward the general store. Tom Russell came from the sheriff's office, stopped a moment for a last word with Doyle in the doorway, and then got on his horse. The rest of the crew mounted. Hoback saw Ives standing with Jeff in front of the *Clarion*, and led his Appaloosa over to him.

"Judge Gimble issued the warrant," Hoback said. "No bail. The boys are spending the night in the poky. The judge set a hearing for nine tomorrow morning."

Ives took the reins from Hoback and Hoback wheeled his

horse and let it walk away. Halfway into the street he looked back, and then checked his horse.

"You coming?" he asked Ives.

Ives hadn't yet mounted his horse. He was looking at the rest of Anchor, riding out of town with Tom Russell in the lead. Hoback frowned at Ives, then shook his head, and put the spurs to his horse, cantering after the others. Ives still seemed to hesitate.

"Ives," Jeff said.

Ives sent Jeff an oblique glance. He looked beyond Jeff at the newspaper office. Finally he turned to look down at the two-story hotel where Tom Border was sleeping. He wiped his hand bitterly across his mouth and climbed on his horse.

Slumped in the saddle, shoulders bowed, he let the Appaloosa move out in its single-foot gait, making no attempt to catch up with Anchor. Jeff saw him cross the bridge, but at the forks on the other side he did not turn off on the Anchor road. He kept on down the main road, toward the gap that led out of the basin.

VI

Audrey Russell was standing before the tarnished Adamesque mirror in her room, braiding her hair into long enamel-black plaits, when she heard the riders enter the Anchor compound. It had taken until early morning for the fire to burn down, leaving only a heap of charred timber where the barn had stood. Audrey had been too worried about her father to get any sleep or even eat much breakfast. She hurried across the living room and out onto the porch. The riders were all stooped in the saddle with weariness. Dust made a white chalk in the rumpled creases of her father's sack coat. The four men halted by the porch and Russell swung down, his saddle groaning to his portly weight.

"Did you catch them?" she asked. She hated the strained sound of her voice.

Her father spoke with a bowed head. "They're in jail right now."

"Eric . . . ?" She broke off, angry with herself that she hadn't been able to check it.

Russell raised his head to look at her and said heavily: "Yes, Eric was one of them."

He handed his reins to Hoback and mounted the steps, passing her as he went inside. Hoback led Russell's Quarter horse toward the corrals, and Kendricks went with him. Only Fargo remained, looking up at Audrey.

The sardonic façade he showed the men disappeared when he was with Audrey. The varnished shine faded from his cheeks and strain no longer made the squinted grooves at the corners of his eyes. She knew the things in him he never showed the rest of their world—the youthful dreams that had been smothered under the hatreds of the basin, the yearning for acceptance and friendship that had never been answered beyond Anchor. There was a shadow over Cliff Fargo that the basin could never forget.

His father had been Kelly Fargo. Eighteen years ago, when Kelly Fargo had come to the lost valley behind the Barricades, he was running from the murder of two train guards and a woman passenger near Rock Springs. The Union Pacific had a price on his head and the Wells, Fargo guards had orders to shotgun him on sight. With him to Wind River Basin he brought the dance-hall girl he had married in Missouri, and their six-year-old son, Cliff Fargo.

They settled with the Shoshones on the northern edge of the range. For months Kelly terrorized the basin. A bank clerk was killed and the struggling new bank was ruined by the raids on Medicine Lodge. Kelly and his renegade Shoshones struck the stage line so repeatedly that Rock Springs Stage discontinued the service. People wouldn't walk the streets at night and a deputy marshal who tried to track Kelly down was murdered.

It was Calvin Doyle and the Thaynes who finally ended it, staying on Kelly's trail through most of a winter before they finally rooted him out. In the battle both Kelly and his woman died, and only the six-year-old boy was left. The Thaynes wanted to leave Cliff Fargo with the Shoshones but the Indians wouldn't have the boy. Doyle took him back to Medicine Lodge and tried to find a home for him but no one wanted him. It was Tom Russell who finally took pity on the orphan and brought him to Anchor.

Audrey became aware that Fargo was watching her curiously, and she wondered how long she had been lost in the dark memories.

"Audrey," he said, "I feel terrible about Golden. I want to break you another horse right away. Ephron has that palomino colt in town. . . ."

"No, not another palomino . . . I mean, why don't you wait a while, Cliff?"

She saw him frown. She wondered what had made her say that. He must have been touched as deeply by Golden's death as she was. He had broken the horse for her and worked it two years in the hackamore before he would let her bit it. But it seemed to her he had been gentler with horses then.

"Maybe you'd rather have Eric give you the horse," he said.

"Cliff, that has nothing to do with it."

His whole mood had changed. The skin strained at his sharp cheek bones again, giving them the hard shine. "Eric gave me a message for you," he said. "No need for you to go out to Indian Graves any more. Eric won't be there again."

She touched her lips. She couldn't believe Eric had told him about Indian Graves. "You're lying," she said.

A deep color rushed into his face. "Audrey, they burned you out, they killed Golden. Would Eric do that if he cared anything about you?"

"I don't want to talk about it," she said. She turned to the door, but, before she opened it, she stopped, biting her lip. She turned back to him. "Cliff . . . I'm sorry."

He wouldn't look at her. "Forget it."

She wanted to say something else, she didn't know what, and, while she was hesitating, it struck her that only four men had come back. She had been too upset to notice it before.

"Where's the new man?" she asked.

For a moment she thought Fargo wouldn't answer. Finally he reined his horse around, still not looking at her. "I guess the weather got too rough for Ives. Last time I saw him he was headed down the main road toward the Barricades. He's probably out of the basin by now."

She knew a moment's regret. There had been something about Ives she liked. But there were always the drifters on the range, and it always made her a little sad to think of them touching her life for an instant and then passing on, never to be seen again. As Fargo rode off, she went inside, trying to forget the hurt she had seen in his face. Her father was sitting at the cluttered desk in the corner of the parlor. He had been working on the books the night before and had left one of the ledgers open. His calloused hands were spread out on the lined paper. Old rope burns made white scars against the oak-colored flesh. She crossed and covered one of his hands with hers.

"You're exhausted," she said. "Why don't you go right to bed? I'll have a big breakfast waiting when you wake up."

He continued to stare emptily at the ledger. His stooped shoulders and massive bent head gave him the look of a tired buffalo.

"I've gone over it a dozen times, Audrey," he said. "There's nothing more we can sell or sacrifice or mortgage. We've got this one last year. If the market doesn't come up at least three cents on the pound, there won't even be any use making a drive."

She looked at the books, remembering how often she had argued against overextending themselves. But her father had been convinced it was the only thing to do. During her girlhood he had spent the winter months of almost every year in the state capital trying to get the legislature to grant a franchise to the Wyoming Central. He had spent an enormous amount of time and money trying to influence the railroad itself, plotting and maneuvering to get connections on the board of directors. Finally it had paid off and his men on the board had assured him that the track would be laid if the Wyoming Central could be certain of a large enough market in the basin. It was this assurance that made him go out on a limb, mortgaging everything to get the land and the cattle that would provide the railroad with the necessary bait.

The Thaynes had made known their feelings against the railroad but the rest of the town had laughed at Russell's schemes and had called them Russell's Folly. Then the basin got the news that the railroad commission was considering the franchise. Jeff Lee started a campaign against it. His editorials gave a shocking idea of what would happen to their town as a railhead. He painted lurid pictures of Abilene and Dodge City, printing their statistics of killings and violence as though it was happening in Medicine Lodge.

When the first Wyoming Central surveying party appeared in Wind River Gap, the Thaynes fought a pitched battle with them and drove them off. It caused the commission to shelve the franchise and send investigators into the basin. It made the Wyoming Central back off. It would cost big money to go to court and condemn the Thayne land, and the railroad didn't want to start any such litigation until they were assured of the franchise. And Tom Russell was left holding the sack.

Audrey saw that her father's eyes were closed. She shook him gently and he came awake with a start. Grumbling, he shoved the chair back and rose, going slowly to his bedroom. She brushed the ashes of last night's cigar out of the ledger and closed it. She followed Russell to his room and found him already stretched belly-down on the bed, asleep. She pulled his boots off and gently covered him and drew the curtains against the morning sun.

She occupied herself with the household chores until near noon, when a strange rider entered the compound. She saw him from the kitchen and went out onto the front porch as he approached. He was a broad man in a yellow sheepskin. His face was crimson and scaly with a deep sunburn and he had apparently shaved that morning with a knife, for there were still patches of hemp-colored stubble on his cheeks and his jaws were scraped raw.

He halted by the porch, touching his hat brim. "They told me you had a man out here . . . name of Frank Ives."

"He isn't here now," she said. "I think he left the basin."

He bent toward her and she saw his scarred hands close tightly on the saddle horn. "You're sure?"

"He was just with us one night. Are you a friend of his?"

He didn't answer. He sat heavily in his saddle, looking beyond her. Finally he touched his hat and reined his horse around. She saw the Corkscrew on the rump of his horse. It was a strange brand to her.

She went back inside and from the kitchen window saw that he had ridden down to the bunkhouse and was talking with the crew. Hoback came out and spoke with the stranger. She saw Hoback point eastward toward the Barricades. The stranger nodded and headed out that way.

VII

On the morning set for the hearing Sheriff Doyle let Eric and Orin out of their cell about 9:00. Zachary and Sabina had stayed overnight in town with Silas Thayne and his wife Beata, and all four were waiting outside the jail.

Eric saw that the curbs of the town were lined with dusty rigs and the hitch racks were full of horses. He knew the whole range was watching this contest between the Thaynes and Anchor, and everybody within a day's ride had probably come to see the outcome. The courtroom was nothing more than George Ephron's old barn that he rented to the county when the circuit judge was in town. Anchor was already there, occupying two of the rough wooden benches.

Audrey sat between her father and Fargo, dressed in a white calling hat and a green velvet basque that flared with the shape of her body. As Eric passed, she turned, and their eyes met. He felt the heat come into his cheeks, and almost stopped. She bit her lip and looked away.

Judge Amos Gimble came from the back closet that sufficed for his chambers and banged his gavel a couple of times. "Hear ye, hear ye . . . since this is just a preliminary hearing, I didn't charge the county for a bailiff and such truck. If you want a jury trial, I can set it over. You'll have to get lawyers from Rock Springs and all kinds of twaddle."

Eric and Orin had already decided they wanted no jury, and told Gimble so. The judge glanced inquiringly at Russell. Russell looked slowly around the courtroom. Eric could guess what was on the cattleman's mind. Most of the town felt Russell was responsible for Peter Thayne's death, and it had turned sentiment hard against Anchor. A jury trial now would be a mockery.

"No jury," Russell said.

Gimble asked to hear the complaint. Russell made it. Gimble asked for witnesses and got the whole Anchor crew. Doyle attested that he had ridden out yesterday evening to see the burned barn and the dead Thayne horse. It was obviously pointless for the Thaynes to deny the charges in the face of such testimony. Orin stood up. He was only twenty and had a temper like a mean bronco. Eric knew how he hated the way his voice shook when he got mad.

"I want to make one thing clear," Orin said. "Whatever charges there are you got to make them against me. Eric didn't have anything to do with it. He tried to stop me at home and the only reason he come along was to try and stop me."

"The court will take that into consideration," Judge Gimble said.

With the stock that had died in the fire Russell estimated the damage at $1,000. Gimble fined the Thaynes that amount plus court costs and sentenced Orin to ninety days in jail. Orin accepted it silently, scowling at the floor, his fists clenched. Doyle took him into custody, and there was nothing for the rest of them to do but leave. On the way out Eric tried to push through the crowd to Audrey. She saw him coming but she would not stop and wait. She looked toward the south. Indian Graves was that way.

There was little talking on the way back to the gap. Zachary was sunk in a black mood and Sabina was a strange, self-contained girl who had always been an enigma to Eric anyway. Eric had Audrey on his mind. Could her glance toward Indian Graves have meant she wanted to meet him there? About five miles out of town he said he wanted to have another look at the place where Peter had been killed, and cut away from them without waiting for any answer.

They had found Peter's body on the south edge of their range, in the foothills of the Barricades. Indian Graves was two miles beyond the spot. A grove of poplars stood on the westward slope and the red spring blossoms were already beginning to stipple the lacquered green mass of their foliage. Some of the trees still bore the Indian burial platforms high in their branches, and, when he was a boy, Eric had climbed up to gape at the grisly skeletons and take the beads and flint arrowheads and tattered bits of buckskin for souvenirs. Later on, when he and Audrey had started seeing each other against the wishes of both families, the grove had become a rendezvous. Eric waited for long hours and had nearly given Audrey up when he finally saw her coming across the flats from the direction of Anchor. She had changed the basque and hoop skirt for a riding habit and was riding side-saddle. The horse was a bay and it made his throat close up, remembering how she had never come on any other horse except Golden. She halted the bay beside him and sat, looking down. The sun and the wind had put a flush to her cheeks and her violet eyes were full of dark shadow.

"Audrey," he said. "Judge Gimble . . . I mean, at the trial, he believed Orin. It was true. I tried to stop Orin. . . ."

"Did you?" she asked.

The deep bitterness in her voice made him ask: "Why did you come, then, if you think I burned you out?"

She suddenly buried her face in her hands and sobbed: "Eric, what's happened, why are we doing these things to each other?"

He put his hands to her waist and she let her weight come down against him and slid off the horse into his arms. He held her tightly and felt her whole body shake as she cried. The scent of her perfume blended with the resinous smell of the poplars.

"You've got to know how it happened," he said. "Orin was certain that Peter was killed by somebody from Anchor."

"It isn't true. Dad wouldn't stand for anything like that . . . so cold-blooded. You've got to believe that, Eric."

"I tried to, Audrey. I wanted to. But Orin . . . you know his temper. It got to eating at him . . . and then that editorial Jeff Lee wrote, reminding the basin how Fargo always did your dad's dirty work, saying any outfit that would murder should be burned out of the basin. Maybe that's how it got in Orin's mind. He rode off that night. I was afraid he'd do something crazy. I followed. I didn't catch up till he'd reached your place. The barn . . . it was already on fire. . . ."

She made a soft sound. "Take me away, Eric. Let's go away, as we always planned . . . all those dreams, out here in the grove. . . ."

He kissed her. He kissed her lips and kissed her eyes shut and pulled her wet face against his and held her while she trembled.

"They say Chicago is a good place to get a start. How would you like Chicago?"

She didn't answer for a long time. She stood heavily against him, and, when she finally spoke, her mouth was pressed against his chest and her words were muffled.

"We'll never get to Chicago. I can't leave Dad now. You can't leave, either. You know you can't."

He was silent, hopelessly silent. Finally, in a dead voice, he said: "Isn't there any way, Audrey? Isn't there anything you can do to make your dad give up this idea of the railroad?"

"He can't survive without it. Can't you understand that? Can't you people ever understand that?" she asked. He didn't answer. After a long time she pulled back and looked up at him. "Isn't there some compromise . . . some halfway ground where we could meet?"

"Not for Dad . . . not after Peter," he said.

"If we could find out who killed Peter, if we could prove it wasn't anybody from Anchor?"

Eric looked at her helplessly, unwilling to express the futility in his mind. He heard a sound behind him and wheeled to see a rider coming through the trees. It was Cliff Fargo. Leaf shadows dappled his blanket coat in a moving pattern. He halted his tiger-striped roan five feet away. The horse fiddled nervously, tongue-rolling the cricket in its bit. Audrey had pulled away from Eric, and her face was deeply flushed.

"Your pa wouldn't like this," Fargo told her.

"Don't try to make it look like Dad sent you here," she said disgustedly. "I won't be spied on, Cliff. I won't be trailed like a fugitive wherever I go."

"All right. So Tom didn't send me. I won't let you make a fool of yourself, Audrey. How can you talk to this man . . . the burning, killing Golden. . . ."

"You should know about killing," Eric said.

"Stay out of this," Fargo told him. "We settled that in town."

"Nothing was settled in town," Eric said. "A bottleneck cartridge that didn't fit your gun. What does that prove?"

"It proves you're Jeff Lee's parrot. Read those words in his paper and you sound just like him. Talk about proving . . . you ain't got no more proof than he did."

"The proof's in the blood, Fargo."

"Blood?"

"Kelly Fargo's blood. It's in you, Fargo, and it's showing."

Fargo made a soft, womanish sound and slid off his horse. He started toward Eric. Audrey stepped between them, going quickly to Fargo. It stopped him. She touched his arm. The anger and disgust were gone from her face and in it was a soft plea.

"This is the last thing you want, and you know it. Please go away, Cliff. You'll only make things worse. There's nothing you can do here."

Fargo seemed to have forgotten the other man. Eric had the feeling of something surrounding the two people, a strange spell, enclosing them, cutting them off from him so that he wasn't even there, something from their past, from their childhood. The only sound was the roan rattling the cricket in its bit.

"Please, Cliff," Audrey whispered. "For my sake."

Eric had never thought he would see Fargo reveal as much emotion as he did in that moment. Then he wheeled and mounted the roan and spurred it to a dead gallop out of the grove. Audrey watched him go. After a long time Eric said: "You're the only one who could've stopped him."

Her chin lifted a little, as though his voice had surprised her. "You shouldn't have said that about his father. He can't stand being reminded. It's the one thing he can't bear."

"He must be getting real spooky. I never saw it make him jump so high before."

"I don't know . . . I used to think I knew him, Eric. I'm beginning to wonder now. There are things in him . . . it seems I never saw them before. It frightens me."

VIII

The same morning near noon the sun in his eyes woke Frank Ives. The heat sucked molasses-colored pitch from the trees behind him and the smell of it hung as sweet as honey in the still air of Wind River Gap.

It had taken Ives till late yesterday afternoon to reach the gap from Medicine Lodge. He had been falling asleep in the saddle, and, when he reached the first snowslide choking the narrow cañon, he had known it was time to quit. Thought of Tom Border behind him had made Ives cautious. He had sought a sheltered spot in the timber off the road, backtracking on foot for a few hundred yards to erase his sign. It had been a cold camp, without supper, and there would be no breakfast. His stomach cramped with hunger as he sat up, absently brushing the glittering spruce needles off his shoulders. He turned, looking for his tethered horse. He could not see it.

In its place stood Sabina Thayne.

She stood with her back to a tree, a brass-framed Winchester across one hip, aimed at him. He was so surprised he didn't speak for a moment. He was struck again by the haunting face, the wild, untamed look of her. She didn't wear the fashionable clothes he had seen on Audrey. She wore a shirtwaist washed so often in home-made soap that the lye had turned it more yellow than white. She wore a man's old blue jeans, patched with rawhide at the knees, and home-made moccasins of yellow horsehide. She stared at him silently, the same withdrawn silence she had showed at the cabin, the wary aloofness of a woods creature too long away from people.

"You put my horse in a hole, or something?" he asked.

She regarded him solemnly for a moment. Then she said: "Your horse is down by the road. He must've pulled loose his tether. Now git up and put your poke together."

He frowned at her. She gave an impatient jerk to the rifle. He grinned wryly and got to one knee, starting to make his bedroll.

"I passed your cut-off several miles back. What are you doing way up here?" he asked. She didn't answer and he tried again. "You must have been to town for the hearing. What happened?"

She didn't speak for so long he thought she didn't mean to. Then it burst from her. "They put Orin in jail . . . that's what happened. They put Orin in jail for three months." Tears came to her eyes. She shook her head angrily, the tangled mass of wheat-yellow hair bobbing around her face. "Now heist your gear. I'm takin' you to Pa. He kin hold you till we find the rest of Anchor."

"They aren't up here," Ives said. "I'm alone."

She studied him suspiciously. It made her lips look full, pouting. It made him think of a small child, concentrating. "How old are you, Sabina?"

She flushed. "Eighteen. Old enough to bust a bronc' or shoot a man. Now git!"

He heaved the Mother Hubbard saddle onto his shoulder, tucked his war bag under his free arm, and picked up the blanket roll by its rawhide tie.

She let him go ahead of her. His boots crackled against the

brittle second-season cones littering the ground. The red scarps of the cañon were beginning to give off a fire glow in the bright morning light. The sun made a jeweled glitter in the glaring white drifts poised on the cliffs. Those high snowbanks gave Ives the sense of waiting, precariously balanced at the very edge, ready to break free at the slightest touch. He knew how little it would take to send them crashing down into the cañon. All through the previous afternoon, as he had approached the gap, he'd heard the cannonade of avalanches booming back and forth through the mountains.

He moved out of timber and saw two horses hitched at the edge of the road—both Appaloosas.

It made him stop. He could identify his, because of the hobbles. The other one wasn't marked identically. The blue of the chest and forequarters was not as dark, was more distinctly roan, and the spots on the white rump were larger and more haphazard. But at a distance, with both horses stripped, they would have been hard to tell apart.

"Looks like we got twins," he said.

"Peter's horse," she said bitterly.

He couldn't help glancing at Sabina. He knew he shouldn't be surprised at seeing another Appaloosa. He hadn't run across many of them farther south, but they shouldn't be uncommon up here. He'd heard they were originally bred for war ponies by the Nez Percé Indians in the Palouse country, and that was eastern Idaho, just across the Snakes from this basin. But something still nagged at him.

"Was Peter riding the horse when he was killed?" he asked.

She hesitated, then said angrily: "Git your saddle on. You're too danged nosy."

He walked to his horse, disturbed by the thought that had occurred to him. What if Tom Border had come upon Peter Thayne at a distance, riding an Appaloosa? Then his excitement faded. It didn't add up. Peter Thayne had been killed the day before Ives reached Medicine Lodge, and Border had shown up the day after Ives. Dismissing the thought, Ives inspected the tie rope on his horse, found it unbroken. The Appaloosa had probably pulled it free during the night, but the hobbles had prevented the animal from grazing far.

The girl mounted her horse, the gun on Ives all the time he was saddling up. He didn't want to go back to the Thayne place. It would take hours and he had lost too much time already by oversleeping. There was no telling how soon Tom Border would find out he had left the basin, and would be following.

Sabina hadn't moved her horse away and Ives saw his chance. Unless he held its head down, his Appaloosa tended to wheel when he got aboard. He mounted, letting the mare go deliberately, and her spotted rump swung around against the front of the girl's horse before Sabina could back away. The Appaloosa was touchy about another horse behind. She squealed and cat-backed and lashed out with both hind hoofs. One of them caught Sabina's horse on the nose. The animal made a crazed sound and reared.

Sabina fought to stay on her pitching horse and cursed Ives and fired at him all at the same time. The shot went wild and she cocked the gun to fire again. But she went out of the saddle before she could pull the trigger.

The echoes of the shot were still crashing back and forth across the gap. They were joined by an ominous rumble from above. Ives looked up to see snow tumbling down the steep slope from the cliff above. He knew the reverberations must have loosened the slide.

"Sabina!" he shouted. "Get out of here . . . down the road!"

She was lying on her face. She moaned, stirred feebly, but made no attempt to rise. He realized the fall had stunned her, and wheeled his horse back toward her. The slide was building to an avalanche—a white wall of snow that was carrying everything loose along with it, a torrent of rocks and débris and deadfalls pouring straight down toward Sabina.

He knew he didn't have time to get her out of its way. He dropped off the Appaloosa, whacking her rump. The horse bolted and he turned to catch the dazed girl under her arms. He dragged her ten feet to a big boulder that jutted over the road. He dropped her flat behind it and threw himself across her as the first wave of the avalanche reached them.

It poured over them with a deafening roar. Deadfalls shattered themselves against the boulder and rocks as big as a man's head cracked against it and bounced over Ives and the snow poured onto him in a smothering tide.

Sabina struggled feebly to rise, panicked, and he had to fight with her and shout: "Lie still, it won't smother us . . . don't lose your head!"

He got a mouthful of snow and thought he would choke to death. More débris was smashing against the boulder and the weight of the snow built up against Ives till he thought its feathery pressure would crush him. Fighting a panic of his own, sprawled across the girl, he scooped out a breathing space around their heads. It was silent now, a cold, dead silence, as frightening as the noise had been. He didn't know if the avalanche had stopped or if the snow cut off its sound. The girl began to struggle beneath him again.

"Please, Ives . . . please. . . ."

He began to dig out, making an air space ahead and packing the snow beneath him. His hands ached with cold, and then grew numb. He was shivering violently. Finally he reached open air, pulling Sabina out with him.

The avalanche had spread across the road to the opposite wall of the cañon, choking the whole gorge for a hundred yards up the road. Ives saw Zachary Thayne and his brother Silas on

84

horses at the edge of the slide. When he saw Ives and the girl, Zachary drove his horse into the snow, floundering belly-deep through the drift.

"Sabina!" Zachary shouted. "What happened?"

She made a sobbing sound. "You was up around the bend . . . I saw Ives's horse . . . edge of the road . . . went to see . . . !"

Zachary made an exasperated sound and wheeled his struggling horse, telling her to grab a stirrup leather. He hauled the girl out, leaving Ives to make it as best as he could. Half the time Ives went up to his armpits and the rest of the time he spent crawling on his belly. He was exhausted by the time he reached the edge of the slide. Zachary and Silas stood, dismounted, with the girl. She was explaining what had happened. Zachary turned in a fury to Ives.

"Where's the rest of your crew?"

Ives was gasping for breath. "I'm alone."

"That's a lie," Zachary said. "If Anchor is up here for more trouble. . . ."

"Zachary, calm down," Silas said. "If any other Anchor people were up here, they'd've heard the shot, same as us. They'd be here by now. After all, it seems to me this man saved Sabina's life."

"And he's Anchor!" Zachary thundered. "How can you still defend Anchor? You seen Peter, you seen your own kin, lying there with Tom Russell's bullet. . . ."

"Not Tom Russell's bullet," Silas said. "Not anybody's bullet we can point to. And I'm not defending Anchor. Somebody has to keep his head in this mess. . . ."

"Keep your head, hell. I think you want that railroad as bad as Russell does. I'm sick of your smoke screens. Why don't you just brand your horse with an anchor and be done with it?" Zachary swung into the saddle. His curly mass of gray hair and his eyes seeming to burn in their deep-shadowed sockets made

Ives think of a raging Moses. Savagely he said: "Git aboard, Sabina. We'll fetch your horse."

Sabina sent an uncertain glance at Ives, then swung up behind her father. They had to head off the road and high onto the opposite slope, almost up to where the cliffs started, to skirt the slide. Silas held his horse beside Ives. His baldpate glowed with a flush that had spread through his entire face. His slouched position in the saddle made his pear-shaped belly peep from between the edges of his plaid Mackinaw.

"Is he right about the railroad?" Ives asked.

Silas glanced uncomfortably at him, sighed heavily. "I don't know, Ives. It all seems to be mixed up now. Zachary is a conservative. I try to think I'm a little progressive. Maybe that's why we strike so many sparks. Why do you think we came out here, hunting a new land? We left a land that was used up, a town that was dying because the world had passed it by. I don't want to see that happen here. I grant you the tracks would bring some bad elements. But think of the prosperity it would bring. This valley would boom."

"And the storekeepers would get rich."

Silas frowned thoughtfully and pulled at his pudgy red jowls. "It's curious about the merchant mind . . . everybody seems to hate it, but nobody can do without it."

"There used to be a storekeeper in Abilene named Farraday," Ives said. "He boosted the railroad. He made fifty thousand dollars in three years and thought the tracks were the best thing since Levi invented britches. Then came a day, one of the trail crews that had made Farraday rich busted into town on a spree. They killed Farraday's little girl. A couple of days later Farraday blew out his brains."

Silas didn't answer. His eyes were wide, a little startled, and Ives could see that he was disturbed. Zachary and the girl had rounded up the two Appaloosas on the other side of the slide.

They returned, Sabina on her horse, leading Ives's animal. As Ives took the reins from her, Zachary said dourly: "I don't want to find you here when we git back, Ives. I don't want to find you anywheres on my range."

Ives swung into the saddle, asking: "You going on through the gap?"

Zachary wheeled his horse and started off without answering, and it was Silas who spoke. "I came up with Zachary to see if something couldn't be done about these slides. My shelves are empty . . . the town can't pull in its belt much farther."

Ives glanced at the snowslide. "Take a heap of shoveling. Why not pack some of the grub in on mules."

"If a real thaw doesn't come soon, we'll have to," Silas said.

Zachary called angrily from up the road. Silas started after him. Sabina stayed behind, studying Ives uncertainly. He touched his hat brim.

"If you want, we can hunt for your gun," he said.

"Too hard to find. It'll be there when the snow melts." She tucked her head in and pouted. She would not look at him. She made him think of a kid caught stealing cookies. "I'm sorry, Ives . . . shooting at you, I mean. I guess I got Orin's temper."

He laughed. "I suppose I deserved it. I thought you were taking me clear back to your spread and I didn't want to lose so much time."

She raised her eyes. They were dark, the color of smoke, heavy-lidded as a freshly awakened child's. He wanted to explain it to her, he didn't know why.

"I'm . . . leaving the basin, Sabina."

"Why?" she asked.

He started to speak. Then he checked himself. He was unable to tell her. He realized it would make him ashamed to reveal that he was running from a man. He knew he couldn't explain it fully enough to her. It angered him that this girl's

87

opinion should mean so much to him. It bothered him.

"I've just got to go," he said.

She moistened her lips. "Well . . . good luck, Ives."

She turned her horse and kicked it to a gallop. The spotted horse grunted as it struggled up the steep slope around the snowslide, joining Zachary and Silas. The three of them headed down the road. The girl looked back once more. She saw that Ives was still watching. She touched her hair self-consciously, and then disappeared around a turn.

Ives hadn't moved. He was wondering why it should take a girl, a strange girl, to make him see things so differently. Maybe because he was looking at it through her eyes. He had never felt ashamed for running from Border before. He had thought his reasons were sound. He had always mistrusted emotions and revered logic. And he knew he was being logical.

But now a bitter disgust welled up in him. Maybe it went beyond logic. If he felt ashamed before a girl, why shouldn't he feel ashamed before himself? How long could a man run and keep his self-respect? Jeff Lee had put his fingers on it—Ives was running from himself, as much as from Border.

He should have settled it a long time ago. Should have confronted Border in Abilene, when he first heard Border was hunting him. But that had been only two days after the lynching of Border's brother. The death of the hanged man had been too overwhelming a load on Ives's conscience. He had told himself he couldn't be responsible for another killing, no matter what the circumstances. He had run.

Now he wondered if it was conscience that had made him run—or fear. He had never met a man in the street with a gun, kill or be killed. He shook his head hopelessly, unable to sort out the tangled skein of emotions. If it was conscience that made him run, he felt stupid. He wondered if his sense of guilt over Jack Border's death wasn't as blind and senseless as Tom

Border's need for revenge. And yet he couldn't help but feel it.

He closed his eyes and Tom Border's coarse, belligerent face appeared before him. Mean, egotistical, a drinker, a brawler. The blind, touchy pride Ives had seen in so many of the Texans coming up the cattle trails. Most of all the family pride. There had been something fanatical about it. There had to be, to drive a man to seek revenge for a year.

But Jack Border's death was a year old now. Tom Border's hatred had to cool down some in that time. If Ives could only reach him without the gunfight, talk it out. Words had always been his weapon. Tom Border seemed the symbol for everything that had hounded Ives. He had the feeling he could never find himself till he faced that symbol.

He touched heel to his horse and skirted the snow, reaching the road again on the other side, and heading back toward Medicine Lodge. Somewhere, from far behind him in the gap, came the booming crash of another sun-melted snowslide starting to pour down from the heights.

The sun was low when he reached Medicine Lodge, making heliograph flashes in the town's few windows. It made him remember his first sight of the place, the line of weathered log buildings shouldered together along the single street, the lazy creak of hay wagons coming in from the outer range, the hot smell of parched dust and budding grass in the air—the smell of peace. He could appreciate Zachary Thayne's desire to keep it that way.

He knew what a violent change the rails brought. Abilene was branded in his memory. A thousand drunken trail hands turning the night so hideous with their noise that a man had trouble sleeping before five in the morning, the brawls and gun fights and hangings, the dead men he had seen sprawled in the street, the screaming fancy women and the furtive swindlers and the wanted men on the prod.

The same thing could happen to Medicine Lodge. It was the long, dangerous drive across the desert that had kept the basin from filling up. Once they had a shipping point, new outfits would swarm in. What Zachary Thayne had found here in the early days would be lost for good.

As he entered town, Ives pulled his Appaloosa down out of her single-foot gait into a walk. He hadn't realized the tension that was building up in him. His shoulders were stiff; his hand was so tight on the reins that it had begun to ache. He eased himself in the saddle. He looked at the horses racked before the saloon, the livery, the hotel. None of them was a claybank with a Corkscrew brand.

Ives tied his horse in front of the hotel. There was no lobby, just a narrow hall with a stairway running up one side. Under the stairs were two doors, one opening into the hotel dining room, the other marked *Office*. It was partially opened and Ives could see an old man inside, sleeping on a haircloth settee with his sock feet propped up on a nickel-trimmed base burner. Ives shook him awake and asked about Border.

"Checked out yesterday mornin'," the clerk said. "Headed out toward Anchor first off. About three in the afternoon I seen him come back to the forks and take the gap road."

Ives went outside. There was sweat on his hands. He felt like a man who had just jumped out from in front of a freight train. He guessed what must have happened. At Anchor, Border had found out that Ives had already left the basin. Border must have passed Ives in the gap yesterday evening, going out of the basin, while Ives slept in the timber off the road. Then why hadn't Border seen Ives's Appaloosa by the road? Ives could only guess that the horse hadn't pulled its tether and started drifting till after Border had passed.

The momentary weakness passed and only a sense of frustration was left. Of foolishness. Ives wondered what he had really expected to accomplish. Had he actually thought he could talk some sense into the man? He looked emptily into the street. He didn't know. He only knew that things looked different now. He would not run again. And he still needed a job.

He looked up the street at the newspaper office. He closed his eyes and shook his head hopelessly. He mounted his horse and headed out toward Anchor.

IX

It was after dark when Ives reached Anchor. Most of the men were in the bunkhouse. Hoback lay with his arms folded under his head, staring emptily at the bunk above him. Parson was reading his Bible. Quill and Kendricks and Dave Gannett were playing draw at the round deal table beneath the hanging lamp. The place smelled of kerosene and neat's-foot oil and sweaty leather.

"The prodigal returns," Parson said.

"Returns, hell," Kendricks said. "He jist couldn't git through the gap and the town wouldn't have him."

Ives dumped his war sack and bedroll into his bunk. "Truth is, Kendricks, I just couldn't stand to leave such stout-hearted, good-natured, sweet-tempered comrades like you behind."

"Faithful are the wounds of a friend," Parson intoned, "but the kisses of an enemy are deceitful."

"Save a man from his friends, and leave him struggle with his enemies," Ives quoted. Parson looked surprised, and Ives grinned. "I guess you and I read different books, Parson."

"Never mind them, Ives," Hoback said. "This pure beef diet makes them think they're a bunch of catamounts."

Ives went to the cook shack and learned that Sowbelly didn't even have any breadless pooch left. There was some fried beefsteak left over from supper and Ives ate it cold and washed it down with water. When he crossed to the bunkhouse, a man spoke his name from the end of the breezeway. It was Fargo's voice. The ramrod made a narrow, faceless shadow in the darkness. His spurs tinkled as he stirred. Ives moved to him.

"I heard you was back," Fargo said. "I thought we better have a talk."

"Tell me one thing," Ives said. "Would you really have shot Orin in the back?"

Fargo didn't answer immediately. Ives expected the quick anger he had seen before. Fargo's mild voice surprised him.

"That's what I wanted to talk about. I think you and I have started off on the wrong lead, Ives. It began with that business in town . . . Doyle, the bottleneck cartridge . . . you can understand how touchy it would leave a man."

"I made allowances."

"What I should really do is thank you for knocking my gun aside . . . up there at the Thayne place. I would've shot Orin. I got to admit it. Afterward I would've been sorry. It's something a man wouldn't do if he stopped to think. But I was still on the prod from town, and then the burning . . . well, you know what I mean."

"You treat your crew pretty tough sometimes," Ives said. "I wondered why they respected you. Now I can understand it."

Fargo didn't answer. Ives sensed that the ramrod was embarrassed. He wondered how often Fargo revealed this much of himself to a man. Maybe the dark made it easier. He seemed to be reaching out for something, some communication.

"Well," Fargo said uncomfortably, "you saved Tom Russell from a trampling at the Thayne place . . . pushing him out from in front of those horses. He'll be glad you're back. It's all right with me. But there's one thing we got to git straight."

"I understand," Ives said softly. "You're still the boss."

It seemed to disconcert Fargo again. He hitched at his pants.

His spurs tinkled.

"Well," he said lamely, "I'll see you in the morning."

He walked off toward the main house. Ives stood a moment, turned sad by the glimpse into a man's lost needs. He wondered what made Fargo a loner, always on the defensive, guarded, pushing men away when he really wanted to join them. Ives had always felt sorry for the tough ones. . . .

They started for the roundup grounds the next morning. Russell had delayed it a long time, waiting for supplies, but he could hold off no longer. Anchor had a cavvy of about a hundred horses, handled by a pair of wranglers. One of the wranglers was a Shoshone boy they called Nighthawk. Ives didn't know whether it was his Indian name or just the handle he'd gotten because he did most of the night herding. The other wrangler was Dave Gannett's kid brother Jerry. Earlier that spring the crew had culled out about a dozen head too old for cow work and had replaced them with a like number of four-year-olds fresh off the range. Kendricks had spent the last few weeks busting the newcomers, and, though they wouldn't be full-fledged cow horses for another two years, Fargo said he wanted to start their training right off.

The crew woke and ate before dawn and by sunup Jerry and Nighthawk had the cavvy rounded up and ready to move. While Ives was saddling up, Kendricks rode over to him.

"Fargo wants me to help pick out your saddle string," Kendricks said. "Each of us gits six or seven to work with. You kin throw your rope on that little bay with the blaze, that paint on the far side, that blue roan. . . ."

"Those are all ones you've been busting," Ives said. Kendricks gave him an ugly grin. "Whatsammatter, Ives? Afraid you'll git pitched?"

The bronco stomper rode off, swaggering in the saddle. Ives

pulled his latigo tight with an angry jerk. He knew that most of the choosing had already been done, and it was natural that a new hand had to take the leavings. But he also knew any other outfit would have tried to spread the new broncos around a bit more.

Ives remembered how he had called Kendricks down for killing Zachary Thayne's dogs the night of the burning, and figured Kendricks was taking it out on him. Complaining to Fargo wouldn't help. If there was going to be a clash, he knew it was best to keep it strictly between himself and Kendricks. But the only horse he could really trust for work was his Appaloosa, and he would be fighting green stuff all the rest of the time.

Russell and Fargo led the crew out of Anchor, with Sowbelly following in the chuck wagon and the wranglers bringing up the rear with the herd. They moved north across the long tilted grasslands, crossing the gap road. It started out bright, with the sun shimmering in the wheat grass, but by afternoon the sun was gone. The booming crash of melting snowslides stopped echoing from the mountains. Thunderclouds made billowing tiers over the Barricades and Anchor sought a sheltered spot for camp.

The circle mules hauling the chuck wagon knew the first night's camp site from long years' experience, and, as soon as they got within a mile of it, they went into a dead run. When he got them to bed ground, all Sowbelly could do was rein them into a three-hundred-yard circle and let them keep galloping till a pair of riders came up to help stop them.

All they had to eat again was beef, no coffee, no bread, no canned peaches. The hands were grousing bitterly and even Fargo's presence couldn't stop their complaints. Dave Gannett offered to go through the gap with some horses and pack the grub back in, but Fargo said they were already late on roundup, they were short on hands, and he couldn't spare a man for that.

Jerry had planned to let the Shoshone boy do the night herding, but with a storm threatening Fargo made Jerry go out with the cavvy, too. Instead of turning his Appaloosa out with the herd, Ives hobbled and tethered the horse in camp, and most of the other hands did the same.

About an hour after they rolled in, the storm hit. There wasn't enough room under the chuck wagon for everybody and Ives was one of those left in the open. He moved into the timber a hundred yards from camp and rolled up in his slicker and put his hat over his face and tried to sleep. He was so miserable and so hungry for something besides fried beef that he spent half the night cursing his blind, stubborn, illogical foolishness for not taking Jeff Lee's offer of a job. At least the man always had a pot of coffee, and was sleeping like a human being tonight.

Before morning he was closer to drowning than sleeping. There was so much thunder in the mountains that he thought it was going to split the Barricades down the middle. Lightning started a tree afire and it burned so hard that the storm took half an hour to put it out.

Sometime before dawn Nighthawk and Jerry rode in to report that they hadn't been able to hold the cavvy. The thunder had stampeded the herd. The only horses left were the ones staked and hobbled in camp. Sowbelly tried to make breakfast but he couldn't get a fire lighted in the rain and finally he went into a rage and threw the side of beef in the mud and told them to eat it raw.

Ives didn't think he'd ever seen such an ornery crew, when the light came, and they started the hunt. The two wranglers said they thought the herd had headed south along the river, but they could find no sign in the rain, so Russell split them up.

Ives went with a group including Fargo, Parson, Quill, and Hoback. They circled aimlessly till the rain settled down to a drizzle and finally found sign that hadn't been washed out. The stampede had headed southeast, toward the mountains. They lost an hour hunting a crossing in the swollen torrent of Wind River. They reached the mouth of the gap but the herd hadn't turned into the cañon. The tracks led them on south, finally into the foothills, and up into higher timber. The drizzle stopped and the sun broke through.

They crossed a ridge and rode down a steep meadow littered with brown second-season cones. Long bars of hazy sunlight filtered through the spruce and its heat sucked up a pungent steam from the thick bed of rain-soaked needles glittering on the ground. Quill was doing the tracking. The half-breed spent most of his time bending down on one side of his horse or the other. Suddenly he dropped out of his Mexican-horn saddle and squatted down.

"New sign with the herd," he said. "Look like a Thayne." They gathered around and Ives stared at the hoof print in a patch of damp earth.

"You sure?" Fargo asked.

"They're the only ones use them turned-heel shoes on their horses," Quill said.

Fargo pulled the yellow ropers' gloves smooth on his hands. "Maybe the Thaynes have taken up rustling now."

They moved on down, with Quill following tracks. Then the world seemed to drop away from them. They had come so abruptly to the edge of the cliff that it took Ives's breath. He could see the basin far below, the buffalo-grass flats, the green pastures shimmering in the sun, the blue twinkle of Wind River, all stretching eastward till it disappeared in a honey-colored haze.

"Fargo Drop," Hoback said softly. Ives glanced at him, then at Cliff Fargo, a few yards away and out of earshot. "Not him," Hoback said. "His pa. This was where the posse come up with Kelly Fargo eighteen years ago. Him and his woman and his six-year-old baby. The woman had been hit by a stray posse bullet. She died among them rocks. I guess Kelly went a little crazy from that. Or maybe he thought this way was better than hangin'. He emptied his gun at the posse, and then he jumped off the edge. Only thing left alive was the kid. They say he didn't make a sound for two weeks."

Ives looked at Cliff Fargo again. The man was staring off the cliff. His face was shadowed, melancholy.

"It must be a helluva thing to carry around with you," Ives said.

"I met up with Kelly Fargo a couple times. He was evil, Ives . . . pure forty-rod slimy evil. If ever the devil came on this earth, it was him." Hoback paused, glancing at Fargo. "Do you think a man can pass that kind of thing on?"

"That's a myth, Hoback. A superstition," Ives said.

"You've seen horses go bad, no reason at all."

"There's always a reason. You throw anybody out of the herd . . . hate them, suspect them . . . how long do you think it would be before they turn bad? How do you think it is for Fargo, living under such a shadow, knowing that everybody expects you to go wrong, watching for the first mistake, the first slip . . . ?"

Ives broke off as Quill gave a shout. The half-breed had been moving along the edge, hunting for sign, and was about a hundred yards away. They all joined him. He was pointing off the cliff.

Ives could see the horses, pitifully small, unreal, scattered at the base of the cliff hundreds of feet below. The men stared silently for a long time. There was no movement among the carcasses and Ives knew it would be useless to go down. Hoback cursed softly.

"For dust thou art," Parson said. "And unto dust thou shalt return."

Fargo took a deep breath. "Don't look like the whole cavvy."

"Sign say a lot of dropouts along the way," Quill said. "Maybe fifty or sixty drift away before they reach here. Down there . . . looks like about thirty."

"It's curious," Fargo mused. "Cattle will do this. A storm can drive 'em 'most anywhere. But I ain't never seen it with horses. In all my life I ain't seen a bunch this big drift off a cliff in front of a storm."

"What if somebody he drive them?" Quill asked. They all looked at the half-breed quickly. He nodded at the ground. "Those turned-heel shoe. They come all the way down here."

"How fresh are they?" Fargo asked.

"Fresh enough to follow."

"Let's do it."

The trail led them along the edge of Fargo Drop for a mile till it petered out in the foothills, then turned south through scrub timber to a creek. Ahead of them they saw a poplar grove on a hillside.

"Ain't that Indian Graves?" Hoback asked.

Fargo pulled up his horse sharply. Ives saw something happen to his face, squinting the eyes almost shut. Then he jerked a thumb at Parson. The bearded man pulled an old side-hammer Sharps from its saddle boot and rode off at an angle that would take him around on the other side of the grove. Fargo gave Parson time to gain his position, then approached the grove on its thick side so that they would be invisible to anyone waiting in the trees. They saw a trickle of smoke thread its way skyward from the varnished green foliage of the poplars. Through the close-packed trunks Ives saw the camp.

A black horse stood ground-hitched in an open glade. It was unsaddled and the gear lay on the ground. Beside it was the fire and a crouching man. The sun glittered on the yellow slicker he had spread out to dry, and on his mat of ash-blond hair. It was

Eric Thayne.

The Anchor riders passed beneath a pair of rotting Indian burial platforms in the branches above, and moved into the open. Eric's back was to them but he heard a horse snort and rose and whirled at the same time. When he saw who it was, he went for his gun. Parson appeared afoot on Eric's flank, the Sharps leveled across one broad hip. Eric didn't finish his draw.

Fargo drew rein five feet from him. "What're you doing here, Eric?"

Eric's blue eyes were slitted. "Following a drift of our horses. The storm pushed them out of the gap."

"They didn't drift here," Fargo said. "We didn't see no tracks coming here. Why did you come here, Eric? Out of the whole damn' basin, why here?"

Fargo's voice was brittle, edgy. His yellow-gloved hands were fisted tight on his reins and his whole body was held painfully straight in the saddle. Ives had a sense of some great strain building up in him. Eric did not answer his question. He stared sullenly at Fargo and Ives tried to read what was passing between them. Fargo put his hands on his saddle horn and leaned toward Eric.

"Was she gonna be here? Would you tell her how many of her horses you killed?"

Eric's eyes shifted. Ives couldn't tell whether it was guilt or anger. "I didn't kill no horses."

Fargo's rigging creaked as he swung down. Quill dismounted, also, and they walked together to Eric's black. The half-breed lifted the leg, examining the hoof.

"Same shoe," he said. "Turned heel. No mistake."

Fargo went white around the lips. "I guess you allowed we couldn't do no roundup if we didn't have no horses," he told Eric. "I guess you allowed that would be even better than burning us out."

"I didn't touch your horses."

"You didn't have to. All you had to do was git them running good down that pitch and the storm did the rest."

"The storm was over when I reached the drop."

"Ah . . . you admit you was there."

"Fargo," Ives said. "He must be telling the truth. We were only an hour behind him. His sign wouldn't have been so fresh. Some of it would've been washed out if he'd been there during the storm."

"Maybe the horses got there after the storm, too," Fargo said.

"The sign didn't read that way."

"Stay outta this, Ives. You're no tracker!" Fargo looked narrowly at Quill. "What do you say?"

Quill wiped his mouth. He looked at Eric, at Fargo, finally he dropped his eyes to the ground. "It could've been either way."

The strain grew more obvious in Fargo. His arrowhead cheek bones had a lacquered shine. He made Ives think of a spooky bronco, ready to pitch at the first shadow.

"You're coming to town with us," he told Eric. "You ain't getting off with no hearing this time. You'll have a regular trial this time. I want the basin to hear what happened. Every man here is a witness. I want them to tell what they saw before Jeff Lee gits it in his paper and twists it all your way."

"The hell with you," Eric said.

Ives saw a tremor run through Fargo. "They were Tom Russell's horses. You ain't going to hurt Tom Russell again, Eric. You ain't never going to hurt him like that again."

"I ain't going into town with you, either."

"Saddle his horse, Quill," Fargo said.

Quill crossed to the nickel-horned saddle, heaved it to his shoulder, and walked toward the black. Ignoring Parson's gun, Eric grabbed the saddle and started to heave it off Quill's shoulder. Parson cocked his gun but Fargo lunged across in front of him toward Eric. Eric still had the saddle and he swung it around, head high. The heavy rigging slammed into Fargo's face as he rushed in. He made a broken sound and took a staggering step back.

It left Parson free to shoot, but Ives had already spurred his horse at the bearded man. The Appaloosa crashed into Parson and knocked the gun aside as he fired. Eric tried to draw his gun but Quill caught him from the flank, grabbing his right arm and pinning the gun in the holster. Fargo's face was streaming blood, but he had recovered his balance. He jumped across the saddle, slamming a blow at Eric's middle while Quill still held the blond man's arm. It doubled Eric over. He made a screaming sound of rage and pain and went crazy.

Parson dropped his gun and ducked around the Appaloosa to grab Eric's free, flailing arm. He and Quill held the struggling man while Fargo struck again. Eric's resistance seemed to have released all the hatred and bitterness that had been accumulating so long in the basin. They were no longer men. They were a pack of beasts struggling there.

Ives saw Fargo's fist pump three vicious blows into Eric's middle and the yellow-headed man gasped each time and jack-knifed deeper. Ives swung off his excited horse.

"Let him be, Fargo!" he shouted. "He's had enough."

Fargo struck Eric again viciously. Quill and Parson held Eric from bending forward any farther. Eric jerked with the blow but he didn't have enough wind left to make a sound. As Fargo started to hit him again, Ives grabbed Fargo's arm, pulling him away.

Fargo turned on Ives. The foreman's face was shiny with sweat and blood. His eyes were blank, so far gone that Ives had the feeling Fargo couldn't even seen him.

Fargo took a wild swing. Ives blocked it and tried to hit back, but Fargo lunged against him and tied up his arms. While they were grappled, Ives sensed a motion on his flank. He turned and saw Quill. The half-breed had released Eric, had drawn his gun, and was whipping it down. Ives tried to throw up his arm but Fargo had it grappled. The gun barrel hit Ives across the side of the head. The shock of it rocked the world, and then he couldn't see.

He knew when he fell. He was never completely unconscious. For a while there wasn't any pain. He couldn't understand that. There was a roaring in his head and a sense of shock. He was floating above the ground and there were sounds all around him coming through the roar. Then he realized he was still flat against the earth. He hadn't moved at all. He had only wanted to move. He tried to focus on the want. It slid away from him. He tried to think of his hands. He couldn't find them. They were out there somewhere, he could feel them against the ground, but they wouldn't move to his will. He didn't have any will.

The back of his head began to throb, and then hurt unmercifully. He was sick with weakness. He could still hear strange sounds. A grunt, an animal grunt, like a pig rooting in a wallow, and then a mushy thud, and then the grunt again, and the thud. He knew Fargo was still beating Eric.

Ives hated his weakness. Somewhere far down in his mind he cursed himself for his weakness. Consciousness seemed to slide away from him, and then ebb back. A humming noise. It filled his head. He lost all measure of time. The humming died at last and he couldn't hear anything else.

He tried to rise again. His head ached so viciously that he could hardly see, but some of his will was coming back. He got to one knee and saw why he hadn't been able to hear anything. They were gone. All of Anchor had left. His Appaloosa was browsing fifty yards away. Eric's horse stood where Eric had grounded the reins. Eric lay ten feet from Ives. The sight of him filled Ives with sick outrage.

Eric's shirt had been ripped off his body. His face was a bloody ruin, and, where blood wasn't smeared on his body, the flesh was beginning to mottle with ugly purple bruises. Ives understood why Anchor had left. They had vented their rage and after it was gone and they realized what they had done, they had been ashamed. Ashamed to take Eric to town in this condition, even though they might still suspect him of killing Anchor horses. Ives wondered if Fargo had ever been convinced that Eric had run the horses over the cliff. All along Ives had gotten the feeling of something else gnawing at Fargo, working him up to this excess, some personal hatred completely separate from the general bitterness of the range.

Ives pulled his bandanna off as he crawled to Eric. He wiped feebly at the bloody face. It was a futile gesture and he stopped. He knew he could do little for the man here.

He stumbled to Eric's saddle. A stirrup fender was still smeared with blood from Fargo's face. Ives saddled Eric's black, and then hoisted the unconscious man aboard. It took him a long time and left him spent. He used Eric's dally rope to tie him in the saddle, doubled forward over the nickeled horn. He mounted his horse. He was still being swept with dizzy spells. He took up the reins of the black and started toward Medicine Lodge.

X

It was evening when Jeff Lee came awake. It seemed he couldn't lie flat and sleep any more without getting palpitations and he had spent most of the day dozing upright in the disreputable leather chair near the Albion press. The smell of printer's ink and stale pipe smoke and musty newsprint made him grimace. He wasn't hungry but he knew it was about time to join Doc

Cabell for their evening meal at the hotel dining room.

He rose and shambled sleepily to the desk in the front office, fumbling in a drawer for one of his Montgomery Ward collars. They were his only concession toward dressing for dinner. They were paper, five boxes for $1, and after a man wore them once he could throw them away.

Fumbling to button the collar, he stepped out into the walk. The outside stairs trembled as Doc Cabell came down from his offices above. He had been a contract surgeon with the Army until a Sioux bullet in the hip crippled him at the Little Big Horn and he was carried out by Reno's men in time to escape Custer's fate. He was pulling on the cavalry jacket he still wore—yellow piping, eagle buttons, six-inch brass epaulets, and all. His face was distinctly yellow, deeply raddled with seams, and there was a gray fur edging his bloodless lips. Jeff thought it was curious how a man's face turned to fuzz both at the beginning of his life and at the end.

"You look a little gray around the jowls," Cabell said. "Did you take your pill?"

"Right on the hour, Doc," Jeff lied. He hated the green pills. "You ready for that sowbelly and grits?"

"I understand we won't even git that if them freighters don't pull through by the week-end," Cabell said.

As they started toward the hotel, Jeff saw a pair of riders coming down the street from the east. As they drew closer, he saw that it was Frank Ives, leading a black horse with Eric Thayne tied on. Cabell made a rattling sound and hurried out into the street.

"I was coming for you," Ives said.

The doctor was already untying Eric. "Jeff and I are too old to help you tote him upstairs. Let's get him in the newspaper office."

Eric groaned softly as they slid him off, but Jeff didn't think he was fully conscious. He had never seen a man beaten so badly. He'd thought there wasn't much left in the world that could shock him but the sight of Eric turned him sick. The three of them got him inside and stretched on the rumpled cot at the back of the office. The doctor sent Jeff upstairs for his bag.

By the time Jeff got back, Ives had lighted the Argand lamp, setting it on a table by the cot, and was heating water in the coffee pot. Doc Cabell was seated on a rickety chair beside the cot, washing the blood away and cleansing the wounds with carbolic acid.

"Did Anchor do this?" Jeff asked.

Ives was too agitated to stand still. He began to pace in front of the stove, running a hand angrily through his long black hair, telling them what had happened.

"Anchor will twist it all to hell," Jeff said. "By the time the story gets pinned down, they'll have Eric ten kinds of a horse thief and stock killer."

"I know Eric didn't do it," Ives said. "The sign simply didn't read that way. He'd been at Fargo Drop no more than an hour before us, and the horses went over long before that."

"Aside from the other Anchor men, you're the only eyewitness," Jeff said. "I'll print the story as you told it. There's only one way to spread the truth and make it stick. Word of mouth can twist things up till black seems white, but once you get it down in print, it's there, unchangeable, the same version every time you see it."

Doc Cabell spoke without looking away from Eric. "Jeff, don't get so worked up."

Jeff crossed to the type case, ignoring the vague pains beginning to spread down his left arm. "I'll set up a special edition. We'll have it on the streets before Anchor can reach anybody.

How's this for a headline? . . . 'Anchor damned by its own man!' "

Ives stared at him. Jeff could see the outrage in the young man's face, turning it pale. But he sensed something else, a hesitation. He realized what might be on Ives's mind.

"You surely don't expect to go on working for Anchor, after this?" Jeff said.

"No," Ives said. His voice trembled. "I couldn't go back."

"Then do it up brown, Ives. A blaze of glory, the Fourth of July, more fireworks than Anchor ever saw."

Ives began to pace again, and talk. Jeff started filling his brass type stick. Type rattled off the case with a ringing click. When the stick was full, Jeff justified the line and set it in the galley. Ives had not stopped talking.

Jeff snatched up another stick. He was moving fast to keep up with Ives. Too fast. He felt the pains more distinctly in his chest. He began to fight for breath.

"Not so fast, Ives. I can't pull two hundred types a minute any more."

Ives stopped, looking at him guiltily. Jeff sagged against the table, fishing out a soiled handkerchief to mop at his damp face. Doc Cabell was too busy with Eric to notice. Jeff smiled feebly at Ives, holding up the half-filled type stick.

"Maybe you could think better with one of these in your hand."

For a moment he thought Ives was going to take it. He thought the outrage and the excitement had wiped the past from the man's mind. Then Ives settled back.

"No," Ives said. "I'll slow down."

Jeff's mouth went slack with disappointment. "Well," he said. "Before we start again . . . will you fetch me that bottle of green pills in the front desk?"

Fargo and Parson and Quill didn't return to the Anchor roundup grounds till the next morning. On their way back they had picked up a dozen of the horses that had dropped out of the main herd during its stampede down the valley. The other parties had managed to track down a few more, finding them alone or in little bunches, scattered all over the basin.

There were still a lot more to find, but by conservative estimates, with the loss at Fargo Drop, the final tally would leave them with a forty percent loss. It had been bad enough going into roundup short of hands. With the saddle string almost cut in half Fargo hated to face the work ahead.

Tom Russell was too discouraged to pay much heed to Ives's disappearance. Ives had already left once and Russell assumed the going had gotten too rough for him again. Fargo didn't go into details. He told Russell about the stampede over the drop, and of the Thayne tracks found there, but that was all. He was ashamed of what had happened with Eric. He knew Russell wouldn't condone it. He realized Russell would hear sooner or later, and that it would be better to tell the old man his version first, but shame made him put it off.

He had seen the same shame in Parson and Quill. On the ride back they hadn't been willing to meet Fargo's eyes, and hadn't talked any more than was necessary.

Fargo's hands were so sore and swollen he couldn't pull his gloves on. He regretted the beating now. The range would take it as the sign they had been waiting for. They were constantly on the look-out for his father's bad streak to reappear in Fargo. It was like a pressure against him all the time. The expectancy of everyone in the basin—and his own fear that they were right. He knew the black things in him, the moroseness, the ugly moods, the temper he was always fighting to control.

It had been more than the horses, yesterday. Finding Eric at

Indian Graves, certain he was there to meet Audrey again—
added to the dead horses—it had been too much for Fargo.

He was still convinced Eric had killed the horses. The tracks
didn't tell the whole story. Eric could have been with the
stampede during the storm and could have returned later to
make sure his destruction was successful. Or to confuse the
sign. Or a dozen reasons. He had to be guilty. Why else should
Eric fight to keep from being taken to town? He had killed the
horses. Tom Russell's horses. That was the thought Fargo
couldn't abide.

Fargo's blind devotion to Tom Russell went back eighteen
years, to the time of Kelly Fargo's death, when Russell and his
wife Adah had taken Kelly's six-year-old son in as though he
were their own. Russell had even given the orphan his own last
name. Cliff Russell. For a while it seemed to stick. Then the
railroad trouble began, and the people in town started calling
him Fargo again.

Audrey Russell had been four years old when Fargo came to
live at Anchor. A year after his arrival Russell's wife had died. It
had brought the widowed cattleman even closer to the two
children. He had spent a lot of time with Fargo, hunting and
fishing up in the Barricades. He had taught Fargo everything he
knew of the cattle business. He had willed him half of Anchor.
He had stood behind him, against the suspicion and doubt and
old hatreds of the range. He had given Fargo the only real trust
and companionship and love Fargo had ever known in life. It
was why Fargo couldn't stand to see anything threaten Tom
Russell. It was why his mind went blank with rage when he saw
a man hurting Russell. . . .

Anchor couldn't start roundup till they had what was left of
their cavvy together, and they spent more precious days scouring the basin. The crew was getting more ornery all the time on
the straight beef diet. There were fights in camp and one of the

seasonal grubline riders drifted. Fargo knew he was in for real trouble if they didn't get decent grub soon.

Finally one of the riders came in with news that a load of supplies had been packed through the gap on mules. Russell decided not to wait for Silas to haul it out. Roundup was still not started and he could spare a couple of men to get it. He sent Fargo and Kendricks to town with Sowbelly and the wagon.

They got to Medicine Lodge about noon. It was a familiar sight to Fargo—the dusty cow ponies standing along the hitch racks, the hot sun making the sap bubble and pop in the green logs of the new schoolhouse at the east end of the street. The Widow Pierce was on her porch. She always seemed to be sitting there when Fargo came to town. As he passed, he could see her bird-claw hands tighten on the rocker arms and could see the bitterness pouring from her eyes like a poison. Eighteen years ago her husband had been the deputy marshal killed up in the Barricades by Fargo's father.

Farther on, George Ephron stood in the black maw of his livery barn, wiping sooty hands on his rawhide blacksmith's apron. It had always disturbed Fargo—how such a potty, round-bellied, inoffensive figure of a man could express so much hate. Eighteen years ago Ephron's brother had been a teller at the new Medicine Lodge Bank, killed in a hold-up by Kelly Fargo.

It was always that way when Fargo came to town. It didn't seem there was a building or a person in Medicine Lodge that wasn't associated with some ugly memory of his father. And they had never forgotten.

About half a block beyond the barn lay Silas Thayne's general store. It had been the first building in town. The logs were a silvery black with age. The bark had peeled off through the years to heap up against the foundation, and a vagrant wind swept the brittle flakes against the legs of Fargo's horse, like a shower of ashen leaves. He rode past the line of mud-caked mules standing in front of the porch. A pair of swampers were unloading their pack saddles while Silas stood on the porch talking with a red-shirted muleskinner. Silas watched Fargo approach silently. The storekeeper wore his inevitable starched white dickey to hide his soiled shirt front, and his pudgy thumbs were tucked into the waistband of sassafras-colored jeans. Fargo pulled his horse up well away from the mules and dismounted. Sowbelly brought the chuck wagon to a rattling halt beside him.

"Anchor's had its order in for a month, Silas," Fargo said. "How much of it can we pick up?"

"None of it, Fargo."

Fargo felt heat come to his cheeks. He was used to Jeff Lee and Zachary Thayne and some others in town using his last name, but Silas had never done it before. He had always straddled the fence in the railroad question, had been the unofficial leader of the neutral element in town.

"Silas, I know these mules didn't haul in but part of the shipment. We ain't asking our whole order."

"And you won't get it, Fargo. Anchor will never buy anything more from this store."

A sick feeling began, deep in Fargo's belly. He realized that Silas must know about Eric. It was another threat to Anchor. Another threat to Tom Russell. Fargo looked down at his swollen fists. He was determined not to lose his temper again. The whole town was waiting for it, expecting it.

"You can't afford to do this," he said. "Anchor is half your business."

Without answering, Silas turned to the bench beside the door and picked up a newspaper. His fat lips were compressed like an old maid's and his hand trembled a little as he gave the paper to Fargo. It was a special edition of the *Clarion*. The front page was devoted to an editorial describing what had happened to Eric. Frank Ives was quoted directly. It gave the writing a factual objectivity that was in jarring contrast to Jeff Lee's usual old-fashioned rhetoric. Fargo didn't have to go far to see how it would appear to the ordinary reader. The whole tone of the article made Eric's beating seem completely unjustified.

Fargo heard somebody come out of the store, and, when he looked up from the paper, Frank Ives stood beside Silas. Ives had no coat on and his shirt sleeves were rolled back to the elbow. The hair on his forearms was wiry and black, and there were smudges of flour on his hands.

Fargo crumpled the paper contemptuously and threw it at Ives's feet. "I guess you know what they call a hand who turns on his brand."

"It wasn't the brand I gagged on," Ives said. "It was you."

The sick feeling was growing in Fargo's stomach. He was holding on tight. He saw that the scene was beginning to draw people. Doc Cabell had appeared on the upstairs landing of his office across the street. Jeff Lee came from the door of the *Clarion*, wiping his hands on a press rag.

"Silas," Fargo said, "did you ever take a close look at Ives's hands? Hoback says Ives used to be a printer. Don't you think he'd rather work with a newspaper than cattle? Don't you think if he came to Jeff Lee with a hot enough story, maybe it would get him the job?"

"Are you saying he colored his story?" Silas asked.

"I didn't say it, Silas. You did."

"Don't put words in my mouth, Fargo. Ives wouldn't have to lie to git a job. Jeff offered him one the first day he hit town. It happens he turned it down, but he's with me now, and he can have work as long as he wants it. Those are the facts you jist read, down there in black and white. Nothing Anchor can say will twist them out of shape."

"You've got a contract with Anchor. You can't back out of it."

"I tore it up last night," Silas said.

"Silas," Ives said. "Are you sure you want to do it this way?"

Silas shook his head doggedly. "My mind's made up. There's no use talking about it any more. You better keep moving, Ives. Most of this shipment has to start to the reservation by tomorrow."

Ives hesitated, looking somberly at Fargo. Finally he moved down the steps toward the third mule in line, lifting a sack of flour off its pack and shouldering it.

Ives, Fargo thought. *Why did it always have to be Ives?* For a moment things got blurred in front of Fargo. He thought he had to get his hands on Ives. Then he knew how stupid that would be, and he thought he would pull his gun and force them to give him the supplies. Then he knew he would do nothing. He was stymied.

What had happened with Eric was bad enough. If he lost control again, he would damn himself for good. He wondered how much longer he could care about that. Maybe he didn't even care now, as far as the town went. It was the thought of Tom Russell that held him back. It was going to be bad enough telling Russell about Eric. He couldn't add any more trouble on top of it.

Fargo turned and mounted his horse. He sat gripping the saddle horn with both hands, watching Ives carry the flour inside the store. He wondered how much farther into a corner Ives could push him.

XI

Sabina Thayne was in the living quarters behind the store, helping Beata peel potatoes for dinner, when Silas came in to tell them of Fargo's visit. Sabina thoughtfully brushed a peeling from her lap, thankful that her father hadn't been here to meet Fargo. She had been frightened by what this latest outrage had done to Zachary.

Both Zachary and Sabina had come from the gap as soon as Silas had sent them word of Eric's beating. Silas had wanted to swear out a complaint against Fargo, but Zachary had refused. Sabina knew why. Eric swore he hadn't run the Anchor horses off Fargo Drop, and Sabina believed him—but she knew her father held a secret suspicion that Eric might be guilty. Fargo and the other two Anchor men would certainly swear to his guilt. It clouded the issue too much. With Orin already in jail for burning the Anchor barn, Zachary was afraid that dragging this latest violence into court might boomerang, causing Eric more trouble than it did Fargo.

Zachary had been raging, wanting to take the thing into his own hands, ride out to the Anchor roundup camp and settle with Fargo himself. It had taken Ives and Silas half the night to talk him out of it. The next morning Zachary had to return to the gap. He and his boys made their living supplying remounts to the Army and there was a string of freshly broken broncos to run to Fort Washakie. Zachary got George Ephron's son to take Eric's place. Eric was still too crippled from the beating to move from the spare bedroom behind the store, and Sabina had stayed to help care for him.

News of the mule train's arrival had spread fast and soon the store was so filled with clamoring customers that Silas asked the women to help behind the counter. Ives was serving people near the front, and, as Sabina entered the store, she saw him look toward her. She felt a faint heat come to her cheeks. She didn't know if it was embarrassment or irritation. She couldn't understand her feelings for Ives. At first, when he had been with Anchor, she had thought she hated him. Now that he had helped Eric, had quit Anchor over the beating, the hate had turned to confusion. Or maybe it had never really been hate.

Jeff Lee came in to buy a pound of Arbuckle's coffee and got into an argument with Ives. Sabina had moved close enough to hear that it was over Jeff's editorial. Ives had already talked with Sabina about it. She knew that he had tried to be scrupulously objective in his eyewitness account of Eric's beating. She had to admit it had taken some of the color out of Jeff's florid style, but Jeff's interpretation had still changed it enough to disturb Ives. Ives had seen the outrage against Anchor that had swept the town after they read the editorial. He had told Sabina that it brought home to him again the havoc that could be caused by a few words out of context.

"You shouldn't have tied it up with the railroad trouble," Ives was telling Jeff. "You made the whole beating sound as though it stemmed from that."

"What else could it stem from?" Jeff asked. "Fargo obviously didn't have enough cause to beat Eric over the dead horses. He was just taking that as an excuse, settling the bigger grudge."

"How can you be so sure? By putting it in that light you've tied Tom Russell and all of Anchor into the affair, and it wasn't all of Anchor."

"Ives, come to work for me. You can't bury yourself in a store, any more than a bunkhouse. A man with your ability has an obligation to people, like a doctor or a parson. What would a town be without a newspaper? Blind. Deaf. At the mercy of every corrupt politician who wants to keep the populace in the dark, every outfit like Anchor willing to sacrifice public good for private gain. Communication! That's what we're giving them. Where would we be without communication? Back in the Dark Ages. Tyrants. Oppression. The Inquisition. Who is to speak for the people? Who's to keep them informed? That's your obligation, Ives. People need to know the truth."

"Facts are truth, Jeff. Is it a fact that Fargo beat Eric over the railroad question . . . or just your opinion?"

"Dammit, Ives, that's what I mean. You've got a gift. You get to the essence of things. It's your duty, your sacred duty."

"You haven't answered my question."

"All right. Facts. So we disagree on a few non-essentials. . . ."

"Non-essentials!"

"Ives, we can't talk here. If you'd sign on with me, I'm sure I could convince you. . . ."

"I'd be afraid to, Jeff. The way you color things. . . ."

Jeff wanted to continue the argument but the customers crowded him out. Silas didn't get the store closed till after dark. Sabina fed Eric some soup and gruel, and then joined the rest of the family at dinner. Silas's wife Beata was a stout gray-haired little woman in calico, always smelling of flour and nutmeg and fresh apple pie. She spent most of the dinnertime bustling in and out of the kitchen and wouldn't be satisfied till everybody had taken at least three helpings of everything. After dinner Silas settled in an armchair to go over his accounts and immediately fell asleep. Beata took her sewing and went in to sit with Eric, while Sabina and Ives did the dishes.

"You're a strange girl," Ives said, while they were clearing the table. "So quiet."

"Maybe I don't have much to say."

"I think you have a lot to say. The right time. The right place. I like intelligent silence in a woman."

"Is that all?"

He smiled. "You have unusual hair. In some lights . . . it looks almost white."

"It's not white," she said.

"Not really yellow, either," he said. "Somewhere in between. A wheat field in the sun."

He was looking intently at her as he spoke. She felt color come to her cheeks, but it wasn't embarrassment now, or self-consciousness. She wondered why she felt so strange with him. Older. Womanly. It was something she had never felt with the men of her family. They still treated her like a little girl, a kid sister. She knew they loved her in their way, but she had been a part of their lives for so long that they took her for granted, failed to see that she had grown up. If Orin paid any attention to her, it was only to tease. If Zachary spoke to her, it was a warning to stop wearing such frivolous dresses. Since her mother's death she had felt lost in their masculine world.

"Will you tote in the rest of them dishes?" she said. "We got to git started."

As he turned away, she bit her lip. For the first time in her life she was becoming self-conscious about her language. *Tote* and *git* and *ain't*. She knew how she must appear to Ives—a back-country hill girl, cut off from the world all of her life. She thought of the women he must have known in the big cities, Abilene, Dallas, Kansas City. She wished her mother had lived long enough to teach her how a lady behaved. Suddenly she laughed softly. Ives returned with the dishes in time to hear her.

"I've never seen you laugh before," he said. "What is it?"

"Nothing. I was just thinking how silly girls can be sometimes."

Ives was sleeping in the shed room behind the store, and the next morning Silas woke him before daylight. The storekeeper had a government contract to supply the Shoshone reservation at the north end of the basin and wanted Ives to start loading the Indian allotment. After a breakfast by lamplight, Ives hitched the team to the store's big Studebaker wagon and parked it by the rear door. It took him several hours of steady work to fill the wagon. He was passing into the store for a last bag of flour when he looked through the open front door and saw Tom Russell ride up to the hitch rack.

The man was alone. He had on a hip-length buffalo coat. It had been one of the rare white hides once and must have cost a fortune, but now the curly, matted hair was yellow with age and weathering. The long mule-ear tugs on his boots made a soft slapping sound as he walked into the store. He stopped uncertainly, blinking in the gloom. Then he saw Silas behind the counter and took off his hat.

"Silas, I came. . . ." Russell broke off, looking at his hat, curling the brim uncomfortably with both hands. "What I mean . . . I heard about Eric."

Silas put a can of peaches on the shelf. He picked up the turkey-feather broom and began to dust the counter. Russell looked helplessly at Ives.

"Is he . . . is Eric here?"

"You can't see him," Silas said.

Russell crossed slowly to the barrel chair in front of the sheet-iron stove. He sat down, his shoulders bowed. Ives thought he looked shrunken. It was always hard for Ives to realize that Russell was really a small man. It was his massive head and tumbled mane of snow-white hair that made him appear big.

"I didn't sanction what happened to Eric," Russell told Silas. "You've got to believe me. I didn't know a thing about it."

"The way you didn't know about Peter Thayne?" Silas asked.

"You know I'm not back of your nephew's death."

"I thought I knew it . . . once."

Russell looked up, his eyes tortured. "Silas, this has got to stop, this killing and burning, this violence. . . ."

"Isn't that up to you?"

"More than me. All of us. The direction everything has taken. We're pitted against each other senselessly. You used to be the balance wheel in this valley. The fact that you were a Thayne . . . could still see my side . . . it kept things from getting out of hand. You've never doubted my word. Won't you believe me when I swear that what happened to Eric wasn't my idea?"

Silas went on sweeping for a space. Then he said: "Very well, Tom. I'll believe you. That leaves it all in Fargo's lap. You've got to get rid of him. The man's vicious. . . ."

"No, no." Russell spoke in a groaning way. "How can you say that? You were one of the few to give him the benefit of the doubt. He's got to have his chance. There's been too much pressure on him these last weeks, on all of us. We've got to slack off. . . ."

"You mean give up the idea of the railroad?"

Russell shook his head. "I can't do that. You know I can't. . . ."

"What else is there?"

"I mean a truce of some kind. Railroad or not, you want to stop this bloodletting as much as I do."

Ives was aware that Sabina had come from the living quarters. She set a pail of water down near the door and stood holding a mop, watching Russell soberly. Her hair made a pale glow in the dusky room. Russell was staring at Silas so intently that he seemed unaware of the girl.

"Can Fargo keep a truce?" Silas asked.

"I've talked with him, Silas. He's not blind. He wants respect here, acceptance. He knows he'll lose his last chance at it if he goes any farther. He's got decency in him, as much as any man. If the basin would only give him a chance. Can't you go to your brother, get some kind of an agreement from him . . . if Zachary and the others agree not to prod Fargo any farther, I can give you my word that nothing like Eric will happen again. Both sides have to work at this thing, Silas. And as to the grub for my crew. . . ."

"I thought we'd get to that," Silas said.

Russell stood, whipping his hat angrily against his leg. "Use your head. What will you gain by starving me out? I can vouch for my crew now, but you keep them from decent grub much longer and you'll have real trouble on your hands. If we don't pull up, if either faction lets things go on the way they are, we'll have a war in this valley, a real shooting war. It could destroy us."

Silas dusted absently with his short broom. He fingered his pudgy lips indecisively.

"I think he's right, Silas," Ives said. "You let Jeff Lee's editorial blind you to the real issue. You're not the kind of a man to take revenge on all of Anchor for something two or three men did." Ives looked at Sabina. "Eric's your brother . . . what do you say?"

She seemed surprised to be asked for an opinion. She frowned thoughtfully. "I think Russell is right, Uncle Silas. We can't let it go any further. With Eric and Orin out of it . . . seems to me your main problem is keeping Pa and Fargo apart."

Silas began to nod. "All right, Tom. We'll try it. Ives was taking this load of grub up to the reservation, but another mule train should be in shortly and we can hold off till then. Ives can take the wagon to your roundup camp this afternoon."

Russell smiled for the first time. "I'll go with him. We can. . . ."

He broke off as somebody hurried up the steps and into the store. It was Jeff Lee, holding his side and wheezing painfully.

"Ives," he panted. "You've got . . . git out of town. That man . . . Border. One of them muleskinners got a copy of the *Clarion*. Twenty Mile, that's where Border must've seen it. He's come back . . . my office. I played dumb but he's asking around town. Somebody'll tell. . . ."

He gasped and stumbled. Ives crossed and caught him, guiding him to the barrel chair. Jeff sank back, his eyes closed and his face dead white. Silas got a dipper of water and Ives took it and gave it to Jeff in little sips. While he waited for Jeff to recover, Ives tried to make some sense out of what the man had said.

Tom Border had followed Ives out of the basin, passing Ives in the gap while Ives was asleep in the timber off the road. Ives knew that much. Apparently Border had not gone any farther beyond the gap than Twenty Mile, the way station at the edge of the desert where the freighters had been held up. Border must have stopped at Twenty Mile when he could not pick up any trace of Ives. He must have stayed there, talking with the Indians and trappers and settlers who drifted in, hoping to get a lead on Ives. And then the mule train had left Twenty Mile with the supplies for Medicine Lodge. In town one of the muleskinners must have picked up a copy of the *Clarion*. The mule train had returned to Twenty Mile yesterday and Border had seen the paper, with Jeff Lee's editorial, and had known Ives was still in the basin.

Sabina crossed to the front door, looking down the street. "Broad-coupled man?" she asked. "Sheepskin . . . dally-rope color to his hair?"

"That's him," Jeff gasped.

"It won't do you any good to go out back," she told Ives. "He's at the livery now, talking with Ephron. He can see either door from there."

"Ives, what is it?" Russell asked.

Ives didn't answer. He knew he couldn't wait for Border to come to the store after him. He didn't have the right to endanger Sabina and the two men. He was suddenly conscious of the weight of his holstered gun. He hadn't used it in a long time.

"You want I should git the sheriff?" Sabina asked. She had turned and was looking narrowly at Ives.

"It would be too dangerous," Ives said. "Border would see you. He'd know."

His mouth had turned dry. He had always hated the code. He had written a dozen editorials against the barbaric custom that put a man in the street with a gun at his hip waiting to kill or be killed over some word dropped in a saloon—or over nothing at all.

"It's stupid," he said.

"Of course it is," Jeff said. Color was seeping back into his face and he didn't fight so hard to breathe. "You're not a gunman."

"It's an anachronism," Ives said.

"Exactly," Jeff said. "The *code duello* was buried with Louis the Fifteenth. Strike a blow for sanity, my boy. I'll write an editorial about it tomorrow. I always thought the monkeys were further advanced than men. They don't set up these ridiculous codes of honor."

Ives wondered why he was going to do it. He remembered his decision in the gap, when he realized he could run no longer. Maybe a time came when a man had to stop trying to be logical—or stop being a man.

"Ives, will you tell me what it is?" Russell asked. He sounded exasperated.

"Let us try to create some diversion," Jeff said.

"Stay out of it," Ives said. "I don't have any right getting you hurt. Just stay here and keep quiet . . . all of you."

As he passed Sabina, she touched him. He paused a moment, looking at her. He could see she was not trying to stop him. It had been a gesture, a contact. Her eyes looked glistening, heavy-lidded.

He stepped onto the porch. He wanted to quit feeling now. He wanted to quit thinking.

The sun blinded him for a moment. Then he could see Tom Border. The man had already left George Ephron and was coming toward the store. There was nobody else on the street. The only sound in the hot spring afternoon was the irritating drone of horseflies around a barrel of dried apricots on the porch.

Border had on a red wool shirt and the same lye-colored

Les Savage, Jr.

pants Ives remembered from Abilene. His beard was an inch long and so dirty it looked more black than yellow. Ives moved down the steps of the porch and into the street.

"Border!" Ives called. "Isn't a year long enough? Haven't you got things straight in your mind yet?"

Border didn't answer. They were fifty yards apart. Border kept coming.

"You know I didn't accuse your brother of the killing," Ives said. "That mob was ripe for a hanging. You'd spent years building them up to it."

They were forty yards apart now. Ives was swept with a helpless anger at himself for trying to reason with a blind animal. Thirty yards, and Border kept coming. Ives knew the man hadn't been a gunfighter in Abilene. But he'd had a year now, with nothing on his mind but revenge. It was logical that the man would have been practicing what he meant to do. The closer they got to the magic circle the surer Ives became of it. Within a twenty-foot radius it was usually the fastest draw that won, and Border apparently meant to wait till then. And Ives couldn't draw worth a damn.

"There were two hundred people in the mob that lynched your brother," Ives said. "Are you going to kill all of them, too?"

It had no visible effect on Border. Twenty yards. Ives realized how futile it was to go on talking. He wondered if he had known from the beginning how useless words would be.

Ten yards.

Ives had to keep it outside the magic circle, there, where shooting meant as much as drawing. And that meant he had to start it. Border was so close Ives could see the strain around Border's mouth and the white scales of sunburned flesh on his raw-looking cheeks. He could see the fanatical glow in the eyes.

It had to be now.

Sheriff Doyle stepped from the notch between the schoolhouse and the harness shop, calling sharply: "Both you men . . . stop in your tracks! I'll shoot the first one that goes for his gun!"

It stopped Border and Ives. Border had not looked toward Doyle, as though refusing to be distracted, but he must have been aware of the sawed-off Smith glittering in the sheriff's hand. There was a moment of suspended threat, while Border stared feverishly at Ives, and Ives thought the man would draw anyway. Then Border's weight settled back off his toes, and his shoulders sagged.

Doyle jerked the Smith at him. "You first, stranger. Real slow motions with the hands. Unbuckle your gun and drop it."

For a space Ives thought Border didn't mean to obey. Finally his hands moved, with a jerky, marionette quality. His gun belt dropped to the ground. The sheriff told him to back off five steps, and counted them for him. Then Doyle told Ives to unbuckle and back away. The sheriff came out and picked up the two belts and holstered guns.

"There hasn't been this kind of gunfight in Medicine Lodge since Kelly Fargo's days," Doyle said. "And I don't aim to see it start now. I want you both out of town within an hour and out of this basin by sundown. If I ever see either of you again, you'll spend the winter in jail."

There was sound around Ives and he realized the town was beginning to come alive. Doc Cabell clattered down his stairs, George Ephron walked from his barn, people were appearing from the hotel, the saloon. Jeff Lee was beside him, wheezing with relief and slapping him on the back. Ives didn't feel relieved. He felt empty, let-down, a little sick with reaction.

"Sheriff," Jeff said, "you can't make Ives leave. He isn't any gunfighter. He was forced into this against his will. Border didn't leave him any other way out. You let him stay and I'll vouch for him."

"Me, too," Silas said.

Doyle studied Ives narrowly. Finally the sheriff jerked his thumb at Border, asking Ives: "He wanted for anything, anywhere?"

"Not that I know of," Ives said.

"What's this about?" Doyle asked.

"It's a long story," Ives said.

"If I heard it . . . would it change anything? Would I want to hold him?"

Ives hesitated. He had the impulse to ask Doyle to take Border into the saloon and sit with him in a chair and make him listen while Ives talked. Then Ives stared again at the animal blankness in Border's pale eyes, and knew how futile talk would be.

"I can't think of any charge," Ives said.

Doyle studied Ives a moment longer, then shoved his hard hat back on his head with a thumb, and turned to Border. "You . . . light a shuck. Get out, and get out for good."

Border looked down. He looked at Ives. Ives couldn't see much humanity in his sullen face. Border wiped a hand across his slack mouth and turned. The crowd made a path for him as he walked heavily toward his horse hitched in front of the *Clarion*. He mounted. He raked the animal suddenly, venting his rage with his spurs. The horse jumped and bolted. It headed in a dead run for the bridge and Border kept raking its bloody flanks as long as Ives could see him on the road.

Doyle turned to Ives. "You'll have to vouch for something, too, Ives . . . that there won't be any repeat of what happened today."

"What if Border comes back?" Ives asked.

"You can always get word to me," Doyle said. "I saw you through my window today. Next time everybody in town will know what Border's here for. It's the only way I can let you stay. Your word that you won't have a shoot-out with Border in this town."

Over the heads of the crowd Ives saw Sabina, standing on the steps of the store. She had a hand to her throat and her lips were parted, full, vividly red. Ives wanted to stay here. For the first time he realized that. For the first time in a year he felt that he belonged somewhere.

"All right, Doyle. You have my word."

XII

Tom Border kept his horse in a run for several miles beyond the bridge till he felt it begin to shudder and stumble beneath him. Then he pulled it down and let it walk for a while. He hadn't been in such a blind rage since Abilene, when he'd first learned that Ives's editorial had set the lynch mob on his brother. It turned his brain to cotton and it was hard to cipher things out.

It had never occurred to him how strange it was that he could follow such a vengeance trail for so long. He had never bothered to question his feelings. If a man was thirsty, he got drunk. If he was hungry, he ate. If he wanted to get a man, he got him. He still turned mean with hate whenever he thought of Ives, and that was enough for him.

It seemed to be a family thing. About the only real ties he'd ever had were with his family. They had lived alone in the brush all his life, fifty miles from the nearest town, twenty from the nearest neighbor. That meant a fight to survive, most of their waking hours. They had fought the Indians, and the Mexicans, and the rustlers, and the Yankees. They had fought the droughts and blizzards and tick fever and drops in the beef market. Maybe such a struggle pulled people closer than ordinary families. When Border's old man had been shot to death by a Mexican, Border and his brother had spent three months hunting the

Mexican down, and had burned his feet for an hour before they killed him.

Yet he couldn't say it was actually love that held the family together. When Border was thirteen, he had been full-grown and that was the last time his old man had taken the bullwhip to him. Border and his brother had buried a calf to its neck in the sand and had killed it by throwing rocks at its head. When his old man tried to whip him for it, Border took the black snake from his old man and lashed him so bloody that he couldn't get out of bed for a month.

Maybe fighting so many things made a man mean. It was another thing Border hadn't questioned much. He figured it was natural for a Texan to be ornery. It seemed he was always taking his hate out on something. His pa had hated Northerners, and Mexicans, and Republicans, so Border hated them. And he was everlastingly getting a horse that had to have a mean streak knocked out with a club across the nose, or a woman who had to be kicked around once a week to keep her in line, or a man who tried to take his woman and had to be stomped on.

When he was twenty, Border's brother had tried to take one of his women and Border had knocked his front teeth out. But they had gotten rid of the woman later and had thrown a big drunk in a Dodge City saloon and had torn things up, the Borders against the whole town, and it had made things right again.

When Ives had killed his brother, Border had vowed before the whole Corkscrew outfit that he would get Ives. If he failed, every man in Texas would know it. If he succeeded, every man in Texas would know it, too. He wasn't going back till he succeeded.

Something was nagging at him now, something about Jeff Lee's editorial. It had told Border that Frank Ives was still in

Wind River Basin, had sent him back through the gap from Twenty Mile, where he had been holed up, trying to get some line on Ives. The editorial had attacked Anchor. That was it. From what Border could make out, there was a big fight in the basin over a railroad, with Anchor pitted against almost everybody else. And the town had kicked Border out. In a sense, that put him and Anchor on the same side of the fence.

It put an idea in his mind. He was still going to get Ives. But he couldn't take a chance on running into Doyle again. He would have to wait for his chance. He would need a place to bide his time, somewhere to hole up and get grub to eat. Why not the Anchor roundup camp? Anchor had already beat the hell out of a Thayne man, and Ives had turned on them. Maybe they would welcome a man who was after Ives's hide. Could be, if he worked it right, they'd even be strong enough to protect him from Doyle.

There wasn't much traffic on the road but he finally ran into a farmer who told him where Anchor had their bed ground. He came upon the camp near dusk. There was no beef gathered on the flats and that surprised him. A campfire winked in the twilight and some hands were standing around the chuck wagon. Border asked for the ramrod and one of the men pointed to a figure unsaddling a tiger-striped roan, and said his name was Fargo. As Border crossed over, he saw that Fargo was standing loose-jointed with weariness, lather from his horse caked whitely on his jeans.

"I hear you're hiring," Border said.

Fargo turned. Border saw that he was about as narrow between the eyes as an Indian tomahawk. Border hated jaspers with close-set eyes.

Fargo looked at Border's hands, at his dally rope, at the rigging on his saddle. Fargo looked at the caked blood on the clay-bank's flanks and his face didn't change expression.

"A short rope and a rim-fire saddle," Fargo said. "That looks like Texas."

Border said truculently: "You ag'in' Texas?"

"Not especially. Can you take a straight beef diet?"

"If I git coffee to wash it down."

"Not even coffee. Our grub has been held up." Fargo looked at the bloody claybank again. "You'll need a string from our cavvy. You can't treat our horses that way."

"I don't usually use my gut hooks," Border said. "I just had trouble fording the river."

There was still wariness in Fargo's eyes, suspicion. Border decided to play it close to the vest. Maybe Anchor hated Ives enough to protect him, maybe they didn't. There wasn't any use letting Fargo know his true identity till he found out for sure.

"All right," Fargo said. "You're on."

Fargo heaved his saddle off the roan and carried it toward the fire. A pair of hands joined him. One of them was a swaggering youngster in a pair of shotgun chaps. The other was a dark-faced half-breed. Border hated half-breeds because they were part Indian, and he hated Indians.

"We're getting sick of eating like a damn' redskin," the one in the shotguns told Fargo. "It takes coffee to pry a man's eyes open in the morning. It takes bread to stick to his ribs. All that beef does is lie there in your belly and snap at you. I been eating so much back fat I'm sweating straight leaf lard."

"Kendricks," Fargo said, "my craw is full to the top with your grousing. Tom Russell's in town now. He'll get our grub."

"Will he?" Kendricks asked sarcastically. It must have struck home, because Fargo didn't answer. He sent Kendricks a baleful look and dropped his saddle heavily on the ground by the fire. Kendricks put his hands on his hips. It gave him an arrogant, sway-backed stance. "I tell you what, Fargo. If Ives is working for Silas now like you say, he'll probably be bringing that Indian shipment north to the reservation. That wagonload of grub should be ours. You send some of us out to git it . . . what can Ives do?"

"Will you shut up?" Fargo said savagely. "I promised Russell there wouldn't be no more trouble. That goes for you and all the rest of the crew. If we have to live on beef the rest of the year, we'll do it. I don't want to hear no more, Kendricks."

Kendricks frowned petulantly and stalked off, followed by the silent half-breed. Border had meant to unsaddle his horse, but this new twist made him think about Ives coming north with the Indian supplies. He hadn't hoped for his chance so soon. He removed only his saddle gun and his bedroll.

They had short ribs and T-bones for dinner that night. As ravenous as he was, Border had to admit a man would get mighty tired of such a diet after several weeks. He could see what a bad temper the whole crew was in. Everybody was as touchy as a cow with heel flies, ready to pop off the handle at the slightest provocation. Border tried to question some of them about what route Ives would be taking north, but they were all too proddy to talk much.

After dinner Border saw Kendricks and the half-breed over by the chuck wagon, talking sullenly together. Kendricks motioned to the horses. There was a line of twenty feet tied to a pair of trees with about a dozen animals hitched to it, including Border's roan. Two of them were still saddled as was Border's roan and he wondered if they belonged to Kendricks and the half-breed. It made him suspicious. It kept him awake after the others turned in.

When the fire had died to a dim glow and the men were snoring in their bedrolls, Border saw Kendricks roll out of his blankets, fully dressed, except for his boots. Carrying these, Kendricks sneaked out of camp. The half-breed followed him a moment later. Border heard the faint creak of leather, the sound of their horses moving away.

Border had given his short gun up in town, but he still had his Spencer. It was one of the old ones they called an Indian Model, in its boot was by his blankets. He took the gun, his bedroll, and his boots, and walked in his socks to his horse, hitched to the rope line. He was almost certain that Kendricks and the half-breed meant to take that grub from the storekeeper's wagon. And Ives would be there.

Ives and Russell reached Long Grade after dark. Ives snapped the reins and the team leaned into their collars. The drop-tongue front gear wheeled into the turn and the big red Studebaker wagon groaned as it started up the grade.

Silas had been disturbed about Ives's leaving town so soon after Border. But the Anchor camp was in the opposite direction from the one Border had taken, and Tom Russell made doubly certain by following Border's track for a couple of miles and assuring himself that the man had headed toward the gap and had not doubled back. The country was too flat for Border to see the wagon leave town at such a distance, and it allayed Silas's apprehension.

Russell hitched his Quarter horse to the tailgate and sat up front beside Ives. They had talked a lot before reaching Long Grade. Russell had admitted how overextended he was, how he stood to lose everything if he didn't get the railroad through by next year. He told Ives about Audrey and Eric. It had been a shock to him, when he first found out they were in love, a deep disappointment. He had tried to be sensible about it, but the Thaynes had opposed him so bitterly, had caused him so much grief and trouble, that it seemed a betrayal for his own daughter to turn to one of them.

"I don't see how it happened," Russell said. "When they were youngsters, it was always Audrey and Cliff. They were inseparable. I just took it for granted she was going to marry him."

"Fargo," Ives mused. "Do you really think that would have worked?"

"Don't call him that, Ives. Don't call him Fargo. There's so many good things in that boy . . . if people would only give them a chance to come out. Cliff would work himself to death for me. I've seen him try. Three days in the saddle without a lick of sleep to save a herd from stampede. Fifty miles in a blizzard to find a bunch of strays. And honest, Ives. I'd trust Cliff with anything. Mostly he takes the drive to Rock Springs by himself. Handles the money from the buyer, twenty, thirty thousand dollars at a crack, every penny accounted for. . . ." Russell trailed off, his shoulders slumping. "And all for what? That work, all those years he's given me. . . ."

Russell's voice sounded rusty with defeat. Ives saw how tired he looked, how old. He realized that the man's hope of a truce had been a feeble one, a last-ditch try. It had put the fight back into him for a while, but it was hard to hang onto in the cold night, when all the pressures against a man seemed to grow so overwhelming.

"What if I gave it up?" Russell said. "What if I chucked the whole thing, quit trying to get a railroad?"

"Could you do that?" Ives asked quietly.

Russell put his big head in his hands. "Anchor would go down the drain. I'm too old to start over again. Anchor is for the kids. It's all I can give them."

"Fargo could get along."

"What about Audrey? I can't leave her with nothing."

"Maybe you haven't got anything to say about that. Maybe she'll have Eric no matter what you do."

Russell straightened slowly. "No. Not a Thayne. That's one thing I couldn't take. Giving it all up, admitting defeat . . . just so I could hand her over to the people who smashed me."

Ives didn't answer. The fire went quickly out of Russell and he sank back in the seat. The road shelved up the flank of the mountain, taking them through timber. They woke a whisky-jack and he began screaming and whistling at them from a pine top. They forded Wind River where copper-colored water birch stood in the mucky bottoms. Ives heard a grouse start its muffled hooting deep in the woods. It had always reminded him of a distant train.

The moon rose behind the timber and the Long Grade road was mottled with long streaks of yellow light and patches of black shadow. The wagon was passing through one of the sections of shadow, so dense that Ives could hardly see Russell beside him, when there was a sound from the slope on their left flank. Ives heard the slither of hoofs in a deep bed of needles, the brittle roar of horses breaking through a chokecherry thicket—and then two riders appeared ahead on the road. They were clearly visible in the moonlight, though the wagon was still lost in darkness. Ives recognized one of the horsebackers as Quill, the other as Kendricks. They both had Winchesters across their saddle bows.

"Pull up!" Kendricks called. "You ain't going any farther!"

Russell started to shout: "Kendricks, don't be a damn' fool. . . ."

At that moment they reached the edge of moonlight and a shot smashed into Russell's voice, drowning him out. Ives heard the bullet strike the wagon behind him. Echoes multiplied the shot, running through the timber in shattering waves, and it panicked the horses. They bolted directly for the riders. It jolted Ives back in the seat so hard he almost pitched out, and he lost the reins.

Kendricks spurred out of the way. Quill had to rear his animal at the very edge of the road to keep from being pushed over the cliff. The reins had caught on the double-tree in front of the axle, and, as the wagon raced between the two riders, Ives went to one knee on the footboards, trying to reach the dancing ribbons. The wagon was going full tilt by then, bouncing and yawing so much that it almost threw him off.

The shots were still coming. Ives got hold of the reins in the same moment that a bullet struck one of the team. It was the off horse, screaming and stumbling, pulling the wagon in a slewing arc toward the drop-off on the right side of the road.

"I can't stop her!" Ives shouted. "Jump!"

He felt the wagon begin to tip and he threw himself off. He struck on his feet and tried to run, but his momentum was too great. He let himself pitch into a bronco buster's fall, taking the shock with outspread arms and slack body. He flopped into a chokecherry thicket and came belly up in time to see that Russell hadn't made it.

The wagon had thrown the man beneath it on the shoulder of the road. When Ives saw it, the front end of the rig was rolling over Russell's legs. Russell's scream rang out above the crash of breaking wood and the wild thrashing of horses.

Then the wagon was gone, rolling on over the edge onto the steep drop-off, pulling the team with it. There was a lot of noise, the scream of horses, the rattle of spilling tinned goods, the shriek of cracking wood—growing farther and farther away as the rig tumbled down into the deep cañon. It struck bottom with a distant crash that seemed to make the mountain tremble.

As the final echoes died, Ives could hear the tattoo of running horses, fading swiftly down the road. Kendricks and Quill, afraid to face what they had done, knowing the wagon wouldn't do them any good now. Ives knew they hadn't done the shooting. It had been a third man, bushwhacking from the timber somewhere above.

Ives saw that Russell lay in the shadow of the embankment on the shoulder of the road. He was only a dim shape to Ives and would be invisible from any distance if he did not move. And the chokecherry bushes into which Ives had rolled screened him from above. Chances were that the bushwhacker couldn't see either of them.

"Tom," Ives called softly. "Don't move . . . don't talk."

There was buckbrush growing on the shoulder. Ives kept it between him and the slope, crawling on his belly toward Russell. The man was breathing feebly when Ives reached him.

"That bushwhacker may be coming down to check," Ives said. "We've got to get you out of here. Can you move?"

"Not my legs, Ives. I can't feel anything in my legs."

Ives knew it was probably shock. The pain would come later. He pulled aside the white buffalo coat. The pants were torn and bloody. Ives went sick with anger. He trembled with the impulse to go after the man who had done this. But he couldn't leave Russell helpless.

The only way out was down the drop-off. It was steep, but not vertical, and there was enough growth to give footholds. Ives pulled Russell gently to the edge, got beneath him, and began working downward. They were hidden almost immediately from above by the angle of the incline and the deep shadows.

It was several hundred feet down and Ives was supporting most of Russell's weight all the way. By the time they got to the bottom, Ives was sweating and shaking from strain. The wagon was a hundred feet away, a mass of wreckage. Ives couldn't detect any movement in the team, or hear any sound, and knew both horses must be dead.

"Tom," he said. "I can't do anything for you here. I've got to carry you out."

Russell was moaning softly, going deeper into shock. "I can't understand it . . . Kendricks . . . Anchor. . . ."

"I don't think they knew you were with me," Ives said. "They probably didn't even recognize you when we hit that moonlight. Everything was happening too fast. Grit your teeth now. I'm going to lift. Everything's going to be all right, Tom."

"Don't fool an old man, Ives. The way that wagon come across my legs, they must be smashed all to hell."

XIII

The next morning Fargo found that Tom Border was not in camp. It didn't surprise Fargo. The man had looked like a tough customer. There was always some drifter signing on for a night just to get a meal, and sneaking away before sunup. It riled Fargo, but there was too much work ahead to let it stay in his mind for long.

He figured they had fetched back as much of the stampeded cavvy as they were going to get, and didn't want to delay roundup any longer. He rousted the crew out. Kendricks was particularly hard to wake, and Fargo finally kicked a hot coal under his blankets.

He knew Kendricks would hate him for the rest of the day, but it wasn't anything new. Some of the men had been with Anchor as long as he could remember, but Fargo had never felt close to any of them. The barrier was always there, his name, the memories. They would stand behind him in a fight against anybody else in the basin because they were good cowmen and he represented their brand. But he always slept in the big house instead of the bunkhouse, and planted his bedroll apart from the others in camp. He had whipped every one of them at one time or another, but the grudging respect that gained for him was about all the feelings they ever showed him.

When he was younger, he had reached out for their friendship. Parson, Hoback, Dave Gannett—he had made fumbling attempts to know them all better. But he didn't have the key. It always seemed to fall through, to leave him feeling foolish. He couldn't do it all. They had to meet him halfway. And they didn't seem to want to. In these last years he had given up. He tried to tell himself he didn't care any more. He tried to tell himself all that really hurt now was losing Audrey. The only one left to him was Tom Russell, and the way things were going, Fargo wondered how long that would last.

After their beef breakfast Fargo led the crew into the Barricades. They reached timberline by 10:00 and the crew split up, each man combing a section about half a mile wide. It made a long line for Fargo to co-ordinate. He rode the length of it all day, keeping in contact with all the men, picking up what strays they missed.

It was slow work, always moving down toward the basin, each man scouring cattle out of the coulées and off the slopes, picking them up singly or in little bunches. It was Kendricks who gave Fargo trouble. Once Fargo came upon him fast asleep in the saddle, his gather drifting off into timber. Another time he was lagging, and, when Fargo put the prod to him, the bronco buster got so ugly, Fargo thought he was going to knock him from the saddle.

By the time they reached camp at sundown Fargo was covered with a gray paste of sweat and dust, and proddy as a spurred horse. Their gather tallied about two hundred head with maybe forty calves to brand. The crew wanted to eat but Fargo felt just ornery enough to make them do the branding first.

Dave Gannett and Hoback circle-rode the herd while Kendricks and Quill set up the branding fires. Fargo's roan was worn down and he roped one of his favorite cutting horses out of the cavvy.

He cut the first calf out of the herd and worked it into the branding fire. Kendricks moved in to tie the legs with a pigging string and Quill came with the hot branding iron. Just about the time the calf let out its squawk, Fargo saw a buckboard coming up the rough river trail into camp. Audrey Russell was driving, and she was alone.

He hadn't seen her dressed so casually in a long time. A buckskin skirt and one of her father's red wool shirts—looking as though it had been pulled on hastily over her shirtwaist in place of a coat, its long tails hanging outside. She wore no hat and the wind had blown her hair into a tousled black frame for her flushed face. It made Fargo remember the earlier years, when she had worn her father's shirts like a boy, and had spent half her time on roundup with Fargo. As she reached him, she pulled the team to a stop so savagely that the horses squealed and fought the bit. Fargo could see the anger glowing in her dark eyes, the little ridge of flesh around her tight lips.

"Get out!" she said.

He stared at her blankly. "What?"

"You heard me! Get out! You're fired. You're through with Anchor. Get out of here! Out of the basin! I never want to see you again . . . Fargo."

She made an ugly word out of the name. She had never used it before. It held as much shock as a slap.

"Audrey, make some sense. . . ."

"His legs are broken. Both his legs are broken." Her voice rose hysterically. "He's in agony! He'll be in agony for weeks. He might never walk again. Does that make sense?"

"Audrey, I don't know what you're talking about. Whose legs? Will you tell me what's happened?"

She made a muffled, screaming sound and snatched the buggy whip from its socket, lashing him across the face. He stiffened, blinded by the pain. She hit him again and he felt it lay the flesh open across the cheek. When she saw that he was making no attempt to defend himself, she made another hysterical sound, half scream, half sob, and tried to go on hitting him.

But she couldn't do it. The whip struck his shoulder, and then his arm, and then she dropped it and doubled over in the seat and broke into uncontrollable sobs.

His face was covered with blood. He could feel it on his cheeks and dripping on his shirt. He could see again, but the stinging pain brought tears to his eyes. He reached up and felt how deep the cuts were. He knew he would be marked for life. He wondered what had kept him from stopping her. Almost as though he wanted her to punish him—for what he was.

"Audrey," he said, "please tell me . . . what happened."

She was still sobbing, her face hidden in her hands. "You know, you know. Wasn't half killing Eric bad enough? We should have done something then. I wanted to. Horsewhipped you in the street, ridden you out of the basin on a rail, something. Fargo . . . how could you do this, the very same day you promised Dad there wouldn't be any more trouble? That wagon was bringing supplies to you."

"Wagon?"

"Silas Thayne's wagon. Ives was with Dad. Ives carried Dad all the way to Anchor. Five miles, Ives, on his back, all the way."

"Tom! You mean Tom's legs are broken?"

"Yes, yes, yes, yes."

It all fell into place for Fargo. He twisted in the saddle to send a savage look at Kendricks. The branding fires were some distance away, but Audrey's voice had become so loud toward the last that Kendricks must have heard. The young bronco stomper stared at Fargo, his mouth open, his face pale and strained. Fargo whirled his cutter and spurred it at the man. Kendricks made a muffled sound, dropped his pigging string, and ran for his horse.

Fargo reached him before he got to the animal. Fargo dived off his cutter onto Kendricks and they both went down. The fall stunned Kendricks, and, before he could recover, Fargo rose and grabbed him by the neck of his shirt. He dragged the feebly struggling man to the fire. He twisted Kendricks's arm behind him and put a knee in the small of his back. The blood dripped off Fargo's face onto Kendricks's shirt. Fargo forced the man's head over the fire, till the glowing coals were inches away from his eyes.

"Talk," Fargo said. "That's why you were so sleepy today. That's where you were last night."

Kendricks made a muffled sound, tried to twist free. Fargo jammed his face into the fire. Kendricks screamed and Fargo pulled his head up.

"It wasn't no more'n you'd do," Kendricks sobbed. "We just wanted our grub. Silas didn't have no right holding out. How'd we know it was coming here?"

"Who was with you?"

"Quill."

"Who else?"

"I don't know. Somebody started shooting . . . I couldn't see . . . maybe it was Ives . . . we didn't know the boss was with him . . . mother's honor, Cliff, we didn't know."

In a wild spasm he tried to get free. Fargo twisted his arm higher, holding him there, and turned to look at Audrey. She had brought the buckboard up to the fire and was staring down at Fargo in horror. She looked like a woman in a trance. She couldn't take her eyes off Fargo's bloody face. She began to shake her head from side to side. She covered her mouth with her hand and made a low moaning sound.

"Cliff," she whispered. "Cliff. . . ."

He got up. He felt hollow inside, completely spent of emotion. "Get up," he told Kendricks. "I want you to tell this to Tom Russell."

Fargo rode all the way with his gun out to keep Kendricks from bolting. Audrey followed in the buckboard, saying nothing during the ride. Whenever he turned to look at her, he could see her face in the moonlight, stamped with the bitter shame for what she had done to him.

There was a light in Russell's bedroom. Anchor had an old stove-up cowpoke named Tensleep who acted as cook and general housekeeper. He had apparently tried to sit up with Russell but had fallen asleep with his chair tilted against the wall and his sock feet propped on the cold stove. Russell was still awake, however, his eyes sunken and feverish with pain beneath their tufted white brows. Fargo had to jab Kendricks with the gun till the man grunted in pain and finally blurted out his confession. Russell sighed. His whole body seemed to relax and settle into the bed. He smiled.

"I'm glad, Cliff," he said. "You know, Audrey thought it was you. I didn't want to think it was you, but I couldn't help it."

"Even after I'd promised?" Fargo asked.

"I know . . . you gave your word, no more trouble. I feel ashamed for doubting you. But what else could I think? I mean, I couldn't see Kendricks doing that without you sent him. I'm glad it wasn't you, son. It takes a mortal load off my mind."

The talk had aroused Tensleep and he was blinking foolishly at them. Fargo studied Russell narrowly, trying to read the expression in the old man's eyes. He wanted to see the trust again, the complete belief. It wasn't quite all there. Russell tried to smile at him, tried to meet his eyes. Then Russell looked away. Fargo made a savage sound and started to prod Kendricks outside.

"Stay a piece," Russell said.

"I got something to do."

"Not with Kendricks. Leave him be, son."

"After what he done?"

"It wasn't his fault. He thought he was jist backing up his brand."

"Sure I did," Kendricks said. Seeing that Russell did not want him punished, some of the cockiness returned. "Silas didn't have no right to starve us. I didn't know you was in the wagon, Mister Russell."

"You knew I told you to leave that wagon alone," Fargo said. He let his weight settle against the floor. It was hard to hold himself in any more. "Get out, Kendricks. Clear out of the basin. If I ever see you ag'in, I'll bust you open like a sack of beans."

Kendricks hesitated, looking hopefully at Russell. But the white-headed man had closed his eyes. Fargo stirred and Kendricks reacted, backing swiftly toward the door, trying to swagger as he went out. Fargo closed the door after him. Russell's eyes were still closed but he made a motion for Fargo to sit beside him. Fargo took a chair. The circle of lamplight was on his face now, and, when Russell opened his eyes, he saw the cuts. Fargo explained that it had happened in the fight with Kendricks.

"Well," Russell said. "You better git Audrey to fix it. Tell her a poultice . . . coal oil and gunpowder mixed up under a buckskin patch. Old trapper's remedy. Never fester on you."

Russell looked at Fargo searchingly. Something in the old man's eyes disturbed Fargo.

"Tom," Fargo said. "You do believe me? I didn't know about it."

Russell moistened his lips. He looked away. "Fetch me some of that laudanum, will you? My legs're beginning to hurt ag'in."

Fargo spooned some of the medicine from the bottle and lifted Russell's head to feed it to him. He turned down the lamp and sat in the dark with his hand on Russell's arm till he felt the laudanum take effect. Russell began to breathe easily and finally to snore softly. Fargo walked out of the room.

There was a light in the kitchen and he saw that Audrey was heating some water on the stove and opening a bottle of arnica. He sat down at the table and put his elbows on the sticky oilcloth top. She stood at the stove and didn't turn till the water began to boil. She brought the kettle and the arnica to the table. Her eyes were lowered and she wouldn't look at him.

"It's going to sting," she said. Her voice was low, strained. He watched her face, wincing as she began to clean the dried blood off his cheek. She closed her eyes, shaking her head. "Cliff . . . I want to say something . . . I mean, what I did. . . ."

"Don't," he said. "You owed it to me . . . for Eric."

"But I feel . . . I feel so ashamed."

"You shouldn't. It all piled up on you, that's all . . . Eric, then Tom. You lost your head. I've done the same thing. I mean . . . with Eric. I've been wanting to talk with you . . . explain. . . ."

"You don't have to. You can't. I thought I hated you after what you did to Eric. I thought I never wanted to see you again. . . ." She turned away from him. "Now . . . I guess I understand it a little better. Maybe I can't ever really forgive you. But at least I know how it happens. You go blind or something, don't you? You don't know what you're doing, really, till it's all over."

"That's about it, Audrey. I really thought Eric had killed those Anchor horses. Thinking he'd done that to Tom . . . finding him at Indian Graves, waiting to meet you again. . . ." Fargo trailed off, looking at the curve of her back, her hips, feeling an old hunger. "Audrey, can't we go back? Isn't there any way back?"

She did not turn or speak. She stood with her dark head bowed. He sighed dismally and leaned back. He didn't know whether it was the long day or the sense of defeat that made him so drained. He ached all over. Absently he noticed that she had spread a copy of the *Clarion* across the table on which to set the kettle. It had today's date and was a special edition. The headline seemed to blare out at him.

KELLY FARGO LIVES AGAIN

Quickly he shoved the kettle aside and snatched up the sheet. The editorial beneath the headline was Jeff Lee in all his florid, exaggerated glory.

> *For nigh onto a generation this plentitudinous valley has known the blessed peace proclaimed in Isaiah—"They shall beat their swords into ploughshares and their spears into pruning hooks." The wolf has dwelt with the lamb and the leopard has lain down with the kid. Not since the tumultuous days of our youth have we experienced the horror and outrage that became synonymous with the name of Kelly Fargo.*
>
> *When Calvin Doyle exterminated this foul fiend, we congratulated ourselves upon ridding our hallowed vale of such a monstrous Magog for eternity. But now Kelly Fargo's mordant shade has risen from the grave and stalks among us again, like Macbeth's ghosts ". . . with twenty mortal murders on their crowns."*
>
> *I speak of Cliff Fargo.*
>
> *How could it be otherwise? He had the brand of Cain on his forehead from the beginning.* Qualis pater, tabes filias—*like father, like son.*
>
> *There were a few among us who had the temerity, the foolhardiness, nay, the veritable Delphian augury to speak out against keeping this tainted child of rapine and plunder in our midst. But we were laughed at, derided, prophets not without honor save in our own country.*
>
> *If Bacon's God Almighty planted the first garden, then*

Lamb's Sabbathless Satan dropped this first bastard seed. And the Blind Ploughman, in the form of Tom Russell, dug the sinful furrow in which to plant the tainted grain, incubated in hellfire and nourished on Borgia's poison, until the twisted young weed sprouted full-blown among our fair flowers. . . .

Fargo felt himself go cold as he read on. Jeff Lee accused him of the attack on Silas Thayne's wagon, of crippling his own boss in his blind attempts to get revenge on the Thaynes. Fargo understood the look in Tom Russell's eyes now, the doubt that Kendricks's confession could not erase.

Fargo began to tremble. Russell had never looked at him that way before. Russell had never doubted him before. It was the one thing Fargo couldn't take—the look beginning in Tom Russell, the same wariness, the same suspicion, the same rejection he had seen all his life in so many other faces, in so many other eyes, looking at him as the son of Kelly Fargo. . . .

"Cliff," Audrey said. "Your face . . . I'm not finished."

He didn't answer. He had gotten up and was already halfway to the door. He crossed the living room, half running, and got out to his horse at the hitch rack. Audrey was right. *You go blind or something.* He was in the saddle without knowing how he got there and he reined the horse viciously around and spurred it in a dead run out of the yard toward town.

XIV

It was dark when Ives came awake in the shed room behind the Thayne store. He realized he had slept the day through. It had taken him most of the previous night to carry Tom Russell from the ambush at Long Grade to Anchor. There were times when he thought he couldn't make it. But the old man had been in such bad shape that he couldn't stand to leave him alone, even to go for help. After reaching Anchor, he had ridden to town for

Doc Cabell and had then returned to Anchor in the doctor's buggy. They didn't get back to town till nearly noon and Ives had been so exhausted that he threw himself in his bunk fully dressed.

He ached all over now and his feet were so sore he could hardly stand on them. He saw lights in the living quarters behind the store and crossed to go inside. Beata Thayne had coffee on and was keeping dinner warm in the oven for him. He washed and shaved at the sink and sat down to eat. Silas came in from the store and sat at the table with a heavy sigh, putting a copy of the *Clarion* in front of Ives.

"A man never realizes how bad a thing is till he reads Jeff Lee," Silas said. "Doc took a copy out to Anchor when he went back this afternoon. If this don't make Tom Russell do some thinking, nothing will."

Ives read the editorial condemning Fargo. It was rhetoric from a bygone era, reading more like a broadside from the Mexican War. Under other circumstances it would have amused Ives. Now it irritated him. It made him restless. He had been through it, had seen Tom Russell's agony, and knew he should applaud Jeff's tirade. But it disturbed him.

He thanked Beata and excused himself. He got a cigar from the box on the shelf and went outside for a smoke. But the cigar tasted bitter and he threw it away. He saw a light in the *Clarion*'s window and crossed over. He saw Jeff inside by the soapstone table next to the press, spreading ink with a palette. He rattled the door to announce himself, and went in.

"You aren't putting out another special," he said.

"One a week is about all my arteries will stand," Jeff said. "I'm setting up ads for the Wednesday edition." He put his palette down, looking shrewdly at Ives. He began to stroke his mustache and then cursed and looked down at his inky fingers. "Dammit . . . how can I break this habit, Ives? If I tie down my hand, I can't set type."

"Shave off the mustache."

"And lose my virility?"

Ives didn't smile. He shoved his hands in his hip pockets and circled the press. He said: "That was an ugly business with Tom Russell, Jeff. Have you got proof it was Fargo?"

"Who else could it be?" Jeff snorted. He picked up the roller and began moving it through the ink. "You saw Kendricks and Quill. You said a third man was shooting from timber. It must have been Fargo."

"Why? I never saw him. How can we know?"

"Ives, how many times do you have to be hit on the head? When you brought in Eric all beaten up that way, I thought you saw the truth of this matter."

"We talked about truth before, Jeff. Nobody knows who killed Peter Thayne . . . but the way you wrote up the story pointed the finger at Anchor. That same day Orin tried to burn Anchor out."

"You can't claim that what I said caused. . . ."

"Had any real violence occurred before Peter Thayne's death?"

"No, but it was his death, not my editorial."

"How do you know? How do you know it wasn't your words that set Orin off? I read that editorial. 'Anchor should be burned out of this valley.' Those were your very words."

"A metaphor, a rhetorical phrase. . . ."

"I call it yellow journalism, Jeff. And now you're doing the same thing with Fargo. You're attacking the man without any proof. . . ."

"Right where it hurts the most," Jeff said. He had the roller full of ink and he crossed to the press, beginning to ink the form. "Cussed roller . . . so worn at the end I keep getting monks on the outside column." He grunted, bearing down.

"Cliff Fargo's father has been his sword of Damocles for his whole life. He can't stand to have the memory of Kelly Fargo hanging over his head. It drives him wild to be reminded, to know we're thinking about it all the time, just waiting for the bad blood to show. And now it's showing. . . ."

"Bad blood," Ives said disgustedly. "That's a theory you can't prove, Jeff. Will you ever stop dealing with opinions and face facts? The hate in this basin is a fact. If anything has turned Fargo bad, it's that."

"You're always talking facts to me," Jeff said. "A man's got to deal in emotion as well. We're not all mind. We're feeling, too."

Jeff put the roller down as he talked, getting a fresh sheet of paper and fixing it to the marks in the tympan. He snapped the tympan down and rolled the form under the platen. He grabbed the elbow-shaped chill, swinging on the lever. He was growing so agitated that he pulled harder than necessary. The platen slammed down on the bed with a wild clang. Jeff let go of the chill and the platen sprang back up again. He rolled the bed out and lifted the printed sheet off the form, barely glancing at it before he put it aside. He was talking all the time.

"Logic deals with facts, Ives. If you'd followed logic, you would have run from Border the other day. You knew it was senseless to stay and face him. You don't believe in the code. It violated everything your reason told you. Why did you stay?"

"That's beside the point."

"It's right to the point." Jeff was beginning to sweat, and his face looked flushed. He put a fresh sheet in the tympan, snapping it down, rolling the forms under the platen again. "You knew you'd lose your self-respect for good if you ran again. You knew that didn't make sense. It wasn't logical. It didn't fit the facts. But it was what you felt and you stayed. You followed your feelings instead of your head . . . and you were right."

Jeff was making oratorical gestures, puffing and wheezing,

getting redder by the minute. "You got burned once because you let your feelings run away with you and you've been fighting them ever since. I don't think you share the responsibility for Jack Border's death. Border and his kind created the conditions that led to that lynch mob. The only one in the world who really blames you is Tom Border. Are you going to accept the judgment of a twisted mind?"

"Jeff. . . ."

"Maybe you'll never get over feeling to blame. Maybe that's one of the crosses we have to bear. The power of the printed word. Sure it's going to burn somebody . . . if you have any convictions at all. Does this mean you quit writing about issues that affect people?" Jeff shoved the chill again, the platen slammed down against the form. "Should a paper print nothing but ads and obits? Does a doctor quit operating because one of his patients dies? We're human. We blunder. We. . . ."

He broke off, his mouth open. He swayed and passed his hand over his eyes. Ives started toward him, but Jeff turned and stumbled through the rail to his desk in front, fumbling a bottle from the drawer and spilling out some green pills. Ives quickly poured him a glass of water from the china pitcher.

"I'm sorry," he said. "I shouldn't have excited you."

Jeff sagged into the chair, taking the pills. "Nothing. Nothing at all. I wish I'd been setting type. What an editorial that would've made."

Jeff was still gasping for breath and Ives asked: "Can I do anything else?"

The editor sighed and closed his eyes. "Maybe you could finish the run for me. And take it easy on that chill. They don't make presses like old Horace Greeley any more."

Ives hesitated, then crossed back to the rear of the room. His back was turned when he heard the horse gallop up outside. He wheeled in time to see the door flung open—and Fargo lunge in. His yellow gloves and serge vest and dusty jeans were flecked with the scummy lather of a horse ridden too hard. Jeff wheezed and started to rise but Fargo grabbed him by the front of his underwear. "I want a retraction," Fargo said savagely. "I want a retraction of everything you said, Jeff, headlines, right on that front page. . . ."

Ives started to cross the room. "Hold it, Fargo. Let him go!"

Fargo had the underwear bunched up so tight against Jeff's neck that it was choking the editor. Fargo was shaking him back and forth in his rage. Jeff's face was turning white and he was beginning to cough as he tried feebly to get free.

"You said a mark on my forehead," Fargo said. "Cain. I never killed my brother . . . I never killed nobody. You string a few words together and git it all mixed up in their minds. You'll unstring 'em, right out there where Tom Russell can read it."

Ives had almost reached them but Fargo had Jeff hoisted out of the chair, still shaking him, and he swung the editor around into Ives. It blocked Ives for a moment, cut him off from Fargo.

"You can't pass on bad blood!" Fargo was almost shouting now. "It's how you're raised. I was raised by Tom Russell. I'm not Kelly Fargo's son. You got to stop talking about that. Reminding 'em. Putting it in their minds. I'm Tom Russell's son. He give me his name, didn't he . . . ?"

"Fargo!" Ives shouted. He had gotten around Jeff and grabbed Fargo's arms, trying to tear his choking grip free. It was like struggling with a madman. Jeff was making feeble pawing motions, mouth wide in a panicky need for air.

"You got to stop putting those thoughts in Tom's mind!" Fargo yelled. "Making him begin to wonder . . . did he really raise a killer? Talk about Borgia poison. You're the one spreading the poison. . . ."

Ives slammed Fargo across the side of the face. The shock tore Fargo's grip free. Jeff staggered against the desk. He hung there a moment, gagging for air, and then slumped on the floor.

Fargo was already whirling toward Ives. His eyes had that same glittering blankness Ives had seen when Fargo was beating Eric.

Fargo threw himself at Ives, with a wild sound, and the two of them smashed back into the division rail. The impact of their combined weights was too much for the flimsy rail. It collapsed with a shriek of cracked wood and spilled them on the floor beyond.

Fargo was first on his feet, kicking savagely at Ives. There was something insane about the way he fought, something totally animal. Ives shouted as the sharp-toed boots cracked into his ribs, his face.

He rolled over, covering with his arms. He got to his knees. He threw himself against Fargo's legs and grappled them. Fargo fell helplessly back against the sloping frames that held the type cases. A pair of cases jarred off, falling heavily to the floor, spilling types and quadrats by the dozens.

Ives let go of Fargo and got to his feet before the man could recover. Fargo followed him back and swung for his head. Ives ducked, counter-punched. He felt it go home, heard Fargo grunt with the impact. They moved back and forth across the room, hitting, blocking, gasping. It was a constant struggle to keep from tripping on the types littering the floor. The metal slugs skittered and rolled under Ives's feet.

Ives was dazed from the kicks and Fargo's blows. He was fighting more by feel than sight. Fargo missed a blow and Ives blindly took the opening, driving for Fargo's belly.

His fist sank deep. Fargo made a coughing sound and doubled over. Ives slammed him across the head, spinning the man halfway around. He could see Fargo clearly, off balance, unprotected, and knew he had him. He stepped in to finish it.

He felt a type beneath his foot, felt the treacherous little slug of metal slide.

His foot went out from under him and he couldn't keep himself from falling. He was pitching toward the press and his flailing hands caught the edge of the form. It rolled beneath the platen with his weight but it kept him from going onto his face.

He was on his knees against the press, starting to pull himself up, when he saw Fargo lunge toward the chill. The man grabbed the elbow-shaped lever and swung on it with all his weight.

Ives was still gripping the edge of the press. He couldn't pull his hands out quick enough. All his fingers were spread out across the form as the heavy platen slammed down against it.

He heard himself scream. A flash of agony enveloped him. He felt the crushing pressure removed from his hands and somewhere back in his numbed mind he knew that Fargo had released the chill and allowed the platen to spring back up. Ives thought he was going to pass out. He put both hands against his belly and lay doubled over on the floor. He heard somebody make a strange mewing sound, and realized it was he.

He couldn't feel anything in his hands now and he remembered how Tom Russell had been too shocked to feel pain when his legs had been smashed.

It was like looking up through a dream to see Fargo towering above him. The man was leaning against the press, still spent from the battle, laboring to breathe. Ives couldn't see well enough to identify the expression on the man's face.

Fargo looked down at Ives, said something Ives couldn't understand, and then turned and stumbled through the types scattered across the floor. He made his way through the wreckage of the railing. Ives saw Jeff lying face down beyond.

Fargo went to one knee beside Jeff, rolling him over. Ives didn't want to move. He was afraid his hands would start hurting if he moved. He had to help Jeff. He struggled to find some will. It nauseated him to move. He couldn't understand why he was so weak. He got to one knee. His hands began to hurt and he began to fall and he knew he was passing out.

The first thing Ives smelled when he regained consciousness was the carbolic acid. It made his eyes water and he started to gag.

"Can't you put that stuff farther away?" he asked. "I'm going blind."

"I've got to clean your wounds," Doc Cabell said. "You can thank a man named Lister."

He was swabbing Ives's hands with cotton soaked in the carbolic. Ives lay on his back in the mess of types and quadrats and broken galleys. He could see that there was a crowd in the doorway and Sheriff Doyle was holding them back. Ives heard Silas Thayne's voice.

"Can't we do something?"

"Best thing to do is go home," Doyle said. "The doc has it all under control. Ives is in no shape for a crowd."

The doctor started splinting a little finger. Ives clamped his teeth shut against the stabbing pain.

"Where's Jeff?" he asked.

"You weren't out long enough for me to set all the bones," Cabell said. "I wish I had some chloroform to finish the job. Queen Victoria took it when she had her seventh child."

"Doc . . . how about Jeff?"

"The noise of the fight woke me up. I got downstairs just in time to see Fargo riding away," Cabell said. He took a handkerchief from his pocket, jamming it between Ives's teeth. "Bite down hard. This index finger's a mess."

Ives thought he would pass out again. When the doctor was finished setting and splinting the finger, Ives spat the handkerchief out. He tried to sit up.

"Doc . . . don't keep it from me . . . what about Jeff?"

Cabell put his hand on Ives's chest and forced him gently back down. He looked miserably at Ives. In a dull voice he said: "Ives . . . Jeff is dead."

XV

They buried Jeff Lee the morning following his death. They put him on the hill beside Peter Thayne. The whole town turned out. The Anchor people were the only ones missing. The parson read a short eulogy and Doc Cabell planted a wooden headstone he had stayed up half the night to carve.

When the ceremony was over, they trailed back to town. Some of Jeff's friends gathered at the saloon, but Ives didn't feel up to joining them. He went to the newspaper office. The shades were pulled, and he sat in Jeff's swivel chair at the desk, looking blankly at the press. Horace Greeley. Ives closed his eyes. He had felt closer to Jeff than to anyone in a long while. Why was time always running out?

He was still in the chair when somebody tapped softly on the door, and then stepped in. It was Sabina Thayne. She wore a bonnet, stiff with potato-water starch, and a full green skirt with a bustle. Her paletot had a high neck and long sleeves and a dozen hooks and eyes to button it tightly down the front like a military tunic. It was the first time he had ever seen her so dressed up. Even the wild tangle of her wheat-straw hair had been combed primly into a chignon. She saw his bandaged hands, and crossed impulsively to touch him.

"Ives," she said. It was soft, compassionate.

"It's all right," he said. "I got off easier than Jeff."

She looked at her hand touching his arm and self-consciously lifted it off. It had always intrigued him how shy and withdrawn she became after they had not seen each other for a few days. Each time it seemed to be a process of breaking down the barriers all over again—like a man trying to coax a wild thing close enough to hand-feed. The compassion was still in her face, making her lips look full, soft, but he couldn't read anything else. He wondered if she remained such an enigma to her own family. Finally he felt compelled to break the silence.

"You heard about it?"

She nodded solemnly. "We were coming in to see Orin today. We met several people along the road. All kinds of versions. One man said Fargo had shot Jeff. Another said he beat him to death with his gun. George Ephron's claiming that Tom Russell sent Fargo in to kill Jeff."

"It's not true. I don't think Fargo really intended to kill him. None of that's true."

"Somebody ought to tell them the truth," she said.

He glanced at her closely. Her eyes were dark, studying him. She turned away and moved to the bulletin board on the wall. She read the cards stuck under its edge.

"International Typographical Union. Louisville Press Association. Pike County Printer's Guild. I didn't realize he'd been so many places." She paused, then said thoughtfully: "You were close to him."

"I didn't realize how close," he said.

"Yet you and Jeff were always arguing."

He stirred. "I'm sorry about it now. It doesn't seem as important as it did. About twenty years ago, Sabina, the two big men in the newspaper world were H.J. Raymond and Horace Greeley. Raymond thought it was a newspaper's first business to print the news. Greeley thought its function was to print the political views of its editor."

"And Jeff was still writing like Horace Greeley," she said. He looked up, surprised at her quick grasp. She said: "He was still good at his trade, wasn't he, Ives?"

"Plenty good. Nobody can ever take that away from him."

She was watching him gravely. He looked into her soft, elfin face, all oblique shadows and tilted planes. He remembered wondering why time was always running out? He remembered what Jeff had said about being burned, being afraid to trust his feelings. He had wanted to tell her before. He knew he should do it now. She should know the full truth about him. He shouldn't wait any longer.

"Sabina . . . when we met in the gap that time, and I told you I was leaving. . . ."

"You came back," she said.

"I was afraid to tell you why I was going. I was even afraid to tell you why I came back. I was running from Tom Border . . . and you made me feel ashamed."

She looked at him a long time, her lips pressed together. "Jeff told us what happened at Abilene. But you've stopped running from Border now . . . that's the important thing." She turned and walked to the wreckage of the dividing rail, looking at the Albion press beyond. "Now why not stop running from yourself? Silas says Jeff was doing something important in this town. I think he's right. You're the only one who can keep it going, Ives."

He stared at her back, surprised at her wisdom. It was part of her contradiction, girl one moment, woman the next. But it seemed to resolve something in him. Jeff's last speech came back. Jeff had said he would probably never get over feeling guilty for Jack Border's lynching. The way a doctor never forgave himself for a patient's death. But the doctor didn't quit. If he had any convictions, he didn't quit. Something had been washed out of Ives these last days—maybe through what had happened, maybe through his association with Jeff, with Sabina, with the rest of them, he couldn't tell. The barrier was broken, all the vague fears and doubts and sense of blame were pushed back. Sabina was right. Somebody ought to tell them the truth. He straightened in his chair, feeling freed, excited. Then he looked down at his bandaged hands. He sagged back in the chair.

She had turned and was watching him. "You'll need a typesetter," she said. "Is it hard to learn?"

He leaned forward, surprised. It was a moment before he could speak. "It's a big job. I couldn't ask. . . ."

"Ives!" She came toward him. "You can't have any idea what it's like to be a woman . . . a girl . . . in a family of men . . . the kid sister. Cooking, sewing, milking, cleaning. The kitchen, the barn. Up there in the gap, cut off from the world. Never asked, never consulted, back in the corner. Watching this thing tear the basin apart, seeing your brothers killed, beat up, jailed . . . nothing to stop it. You're right about Jeff Lee. Some of the things he wrote made Pa so mad I thought he was a-goin' to kill Tom Russell. It was after reading Jeff's editorial that Orin went out and burned the Anchor barn. You think he'd listen to me? You think any of 'em would listen? Well, now I can do something. I can do something to help, and, if you don't have the gumption to do what you was meant for, I'll git Uncle Silas to buy the paper, and I'll learn typesetting by myself."

Excitement had made her throw her head back like a shying horse. Her cheeks were flushed and her eyes sparkled. She turned and scrambled through the wreckage of the rail, almost tripping on her long Balmoral skirt. She knelt on the floor and began picking up types and putting them in a case. It took him a moment to recover from the onslaught. He got up and went after her.

"Hold on, the types have got to go in a certain order."

He knelt beside her and started trying to pick up type with his splinted fingers. She caught his hands.

"You'll get the bandages all dirty. Just tell me."

She was still holding his hands, but the grip didn't hurt. The gentleness of it was in strange contrast to the wildness he had seen in her before. They were kneeling together, so close their bodies touched. He looked at her lips. He leaned toward her. He kissed her.

She yielded for a moment, her lips flowering beneath his. Then she broke the spell abruptly, pulling away, releasing his hands. She rose and backed off two steps, fighting for balance in the treacherous litter of types. Her hands were pressed tightly against her skirt and she was breathing deeply. He got to his feet.

"I'm sorry," he said. "I wasn't thinking, Sabina. I guess it was the wrong time . . . so soon after Jeff. . . ."

"It ain't that," she said. "Not exactly that, I mean." She paused, searching his face. "Ives," she murmured. "Are you sure?"

"I'm sure, Sabina."

"You mustn't think . . . what I mean . . . this last couple of years, there was a boy, more than one, really . . . they wanted to come . . . courting . . . Pa scared 'em away, Eric even whipped one of 'em. I never actually cared much. They was just silly boys. What I'm trying to say. . . ."

"Sabina, do you think I'm like a whiskey drummer . . . a girl in every town."

Her voice was barely audible. "No."

"I've never been in love before. Is that what you want to hear?"

A flush crept into her cheeks. But she was still tense, ready to jump at his slightest move. He knew what it was now. The wild thing, the wood's colt, too long away from people, too long alone, wary, suspicious, unable to trust. Her eyes seemed more tilted, her cheek bones more oblique. It lent her face the fey expression, the same elfin shape he had seen that first night at the Thayne cabin. It made him realize how slow he had to move.

"You've got to come out of the woods sometime, Sabina."

"I know. It's just . . . I don't know . . . Ives. . . ."

"We've got a lot of time, Sabina. Maybe that's what it'll take."

"I guess so. It's so new to me. Everything's so new to me. And you. . . ." She bit her lip. She lowered her head, suddenly self-conscious, and looked around as though for some escape. She tried to smile. "Well," she said stiffly, "this ain't getting the work done, is it?" She bunched her skirts about her knees and started to kneel again. Halfway down she stopped herself, looking quickly at him. "Ives, will you teach me not to say ain't?"

He marveled at how quickly her mood could change. The shyness, the painful self-consciousness was gone. Her eyes were wide, eager; she was serious as a child. He smiled.

"You go right on saying ain't," he said. "We'll get it put in Webster."

She answered his smile, and then the thought of Jeff must have touched them at the same time, for they both sobered, and she knelt quickly over the types. He stood looking down at the little bonnet on the white-yellow hair. Finally he began.

"That case in front of you is the upper case. All the big letters go in it, the capitals."

She started sorting out the letters under his direction. It was a long job, and, when she was finished, her face and dress were smudged with ink and her fingers were filthy. She would not quit. He did what he could to help her lift the heavy, filled cases onto the sloping frames. Then he showed her the lay of the case, how to use the setting rule, how to fill the composing stick, use the leads to justify her line, set up the galleys. She had quick fingers and a good mind. She badgered him to continue with the work till he gave in and started an editorial.

His hands hurt and Jeff Lee was on his mind. It was hard to concentrate. But her eagerness fired his imagination. He paced back and forth a few times, and began to dictate. It was painfully slow, and she had to keep stopping him when he got excited and speeded up. But the things began to emerge that had been forming in him ever since he had seen the trouble in the basin.

It is time for the people of Wind River Basin to distinguish between Cliff Fargo and Anchor. The two are not synonymous. By making them seem so we have forgotten the real issues at stake. A feud has developed that bears little relation to the problems in which it originated.

Many believe that Cliff Fargo inherited his father's tendencies and was doomed to turn bad. I submit that this is false and unreasonable. I submit that few men could have stood the pressures of hate and hostility and ostracism to which the people of this basin subjected Cliff Fargo. We all share responsibility for his actions.

This does not excuse him. No matter what the cause, the fact remains that he has become the instrument for violence and now for death. I saw Jeff Lee die, and am certain Fargo did not intend his death. Yet Fargo was the cause of it.

That is why he must not be identified with Anchor. Tom Russell and the rest of Anchor cannot be held to account for the actions of one man. When we can put aside this prejudice—when we can forget the hatreds that have obscured the original issue—we will have a far greater chance of resolving that issue.

There is a solution to the railroad problem. There must be one. It is this paper's suggestion that the rails be ended at the other end of the gap. That Twenty Mile—and not Medicine Lodge—be made the terminal point for the Wyoming Central.

XVI

Tom Russell was half asleep from the laudanum when he heard somebody knock on the front door of the Anchor house. Audrey's heels tapped across the living room and the door creaked as she opened it. Russell heard her talking to some man but he couldn't make out the words until Audrey's voice rose sharply.

"No, you mustn't tell him, Cal. He's in no shape . . . you've no idea what it will do to him. Won't you take my word? We don't know where Fargo is."

The sheriff's voice answered: "I've got to see Tom. I'm sorry it has to be this way, Audrey, but I've got to."

They came into the bedroom. Russell was fully awake now. Doyle never wore his hard hat or his stud-triggered Smith unless he was on official business. It chilled Russell. Reluctantly the sheriff told him about Jeff's death.

"I've got a warrant for Fargo, Tom," Doyle said. "I haven't checked your roundup camp yet. Fargo must know he's a wanted man. He wouldn't just sit there and wait for me to come after him. But I figure he's bound to come to you sooner or later."

There seemed to be a smothering weight on Russell's chest. It was an effort to speak. "I thought nothing could ever hurt me more than these legs, Cal."

"Fargo's hurt too many people, Tom. Don't you think it's about time to close the books on him?"

"I ain't seen him."

"If anybody knows where he'd go, it would be you."

Russell dreaded to say it. The thought seemed to take him back a long way, destroying eighteen years of faith and hope and love. Finally he muttered: "North, most likely. Up beyond Wind River. The Indian country."

"Where his pa went," Doyle said. Audrey looked at him angrily. He dipped his head in what might have been apology. Then he took a folded newspaper from the pocket of his butternut coat and put it on the bed. "Maybe you'll want to see this. We got a new editor now. Not as colorful as Jeff . . . maybe a little more clear-headed."

When Doyle had gone, Russell closed his eyes and gave way to the sick, gone feeling inside him. Audrey sat beside him, her hand on his arm. There was nothing either of them could say. Finally he asked her to read the editorial. She didn't want to upset him more but he insisted on it. When she was through, he lay for a long while staring at the ceiling.

At last he said: "I think Ives is right. I think it's time to separate Cliff Fargo from Anchor."

"He didn't say that. He didn't even mean it. He only meant in people's minds. He practically defends Cliff. He says Jeff Lee's death was an accident . . . Cliff didn't intend it. That part about all of them sharing responsibility for what Cliff did. It's true, Dad, so true. . . ."

"But Cliff did it. He still did it. That's all that matters now. How can the people ever stop hating Anchor . . . if Fargo keeps on doing these things and we keep on standing behind him? Ives is right. We've got to go back to where it started. There won't be peace till the basin trusts us again, till the Thaynes forget this grudge against Anchor, till they're willing to sit down and work this thing out. And they won't do that with Fargo part of Anchor."

He sank back against the pillows, breathing heavily. He heard the spurs tinkle in the doorway and saw Audrey look up sharply. Russell's loud voice had covered the sounds of the man coming into the house. It was Cliff Fargo, standing in the door. Russell knew he had heard.

They stared at each other in tortured silence. Finally Fargo took off his hat. He looked down at it, turning it around in his yellow-gloved hands. He spoke in a voice so low Russell could hardly hear.

"I guess I been hanging around quite a spell, trying to work up the starch to come in. I seen Doc Cabell come and go. I seen Doyle. I suppose he was after me. . . ." He paused, as though waiting for an answer. Then, in an even lower voice, he said: "I didn't mean it, with Jeff Lee. You believe that, don't you? I didn't go there to do that."

"I believe it," Russell said in a dead voice.

"And you still want me to go."

"It ain't what I want," Russell said. He bunched the blanket in his fists. "Tell me this . . . should you meet them again, the Thaynes, Silas, anybody, and they cross you somehow, they fight you, what would you do?" Fargo's lips compressed. He kept turning his hat in his hand, looking at it. The tilted position of his head put deep, strained creases in the dark flesh of his jaw. Russell said: "You'd fight back. You couldn't help it. And maybe kill somebody again."

"You want to turn me in to Doyle?"

"I can't do that."

"You want me to go?"

Russell didn't speak. He couldn't say it. He wondered how long he had known it would have to end this way? Had dreaded facing it. Since the beginning of the railroad trouble? Since Peter Thayne's death? Since Eric's beating, certainly. Ives's editorial made him see it clearly. It was for the good of the basin. Russell himself had said it to Silas. If they didn't stop now, everyone would be destroyed. Fargo was causing the hate in the basin. If Anchor was destroyed, Audrey would suffer with it. Russell realized it was a choice he had to make, really—a choice between his daughter and the man he had come to think of as his son.

He closed his eyes. He couldn't look at Fargo. "That's about it, Cliff. Why don't you leave the basin. It would be better for everybody. . . ."

Fargo didn't make a sound. Russell finally had to open his eyes and look at the man. He had seen the same look on Fargo's face before—a long time ago, when Fargo was only ten, and

Russell had whipped him for some childish prank. Only the look was plainer now, branded into his face. Then Fargo's eyes turned blank and his lips parted on a single word, so low and so guttural that Russell could hardly make it out.

"Ives," Fargo said.

He turned around and walked out. Audrey looked hopelessly at her father. She put her hands over her face and began to cry.

Ives got to Anchor about 9:00 that evening. Audrey met him at the door, and he gave her the copy of the *Clarion* he had brought. He supposed they had already heard of Jeff's death, but he wanted Tom Russell to read the editorial and give his reaction to the idea about Twenty Mile being the railhead. Audrey told him Doyle had been out earlier and they had already seen a paper. She said Fargo had been there, too, not an hour before. In a low, strained voice she told him what had happened. Then she took him in to her father.

The first few moments were awkward. Ives could see how deeply Russell was wounded by what had happened. He could imagine what it had taken for the old man to cut Fargo loose. Ives found himself feeling guilty again. Jeff had been so right. The power of the printed word. The cross they had to bear.

"You had to cut loose of him," Ives said. He wondered if he wasn't trying to convince himself as much as Russell. "It was the only way. You'd given him every chance."

Russell looked at his bandaged hands. "I guess you must hate him . . . what he did to you . . . Jeff. . . ."

Ives shook his head. "I don't know. I guess I did for a while. But those words I wrote have got to mean something. We've got to quit hating. This proposal, Tom . . . Twenty Mile for a shipping point instead of Medicine Lodge? What do you think about it?"

Russell shook his head weakly. For ten years, he said, the

whole campaign had been based on Medicine Lodge as the rail-head. The railroad wouldn't go for such a change.

"Why?" Ives asked. "They're businessmen. I've been going through the files. According to a report Jeff published last year, the railroad figures it will cost them sixty-five thousand dollars a mile. Twenty miles less track means a saving of over a million dollars."

"It's not only the railroad, it's the commission you'd have to convince, the legislature . . . a new bill, a whole new campaign, Ives. It would take too much time, too much money. I don't have either left. I can't go through all that again."

"You were alone before, fighting the whole basin," Ives said. "Suppose they were behind you? Suppose the *Clarion* spear-headed your campaign instead of trying to wreck it? You've taken the first step, Tom. You've cut loose of Fargo. Now it's their turn. I know Doyle can be counted on, and Doc Cabell, even Silas Thayne. . . ."

Russell raised up on an elbow, a faint glow coming to his cheeks. "It could be . . . it could be. Silas has contacts in the capital . . . his work with the Indian Bureau." He broke off and sagged back. "Not with Zachary against it. He'll never compromise. He'll wreck every move you make in town. He's got too many folks that'll follow him."

"Suppose I convince him. Would you agree to it then?"

"You'll never convince him," Russell said. "But if you do . . . you'll convince me."

XVII

It was too late to go on to the gap that night. Ives returned to town. He was staying in Jeff's quarters now at the rear of the newspaper office. It had seemed a natural thing for Ives to pick up where Jeff had left off, and nobody had actually opposed it. But the city council thought some official action should be taken, so they had Jeff's estate put in probate, and drew up a petition for the press and other necessary equipment to be assigned to Ives. That was as far as it could go for three months, at which time Judge Gimble would reach Medicine Lodge again on his circuit. In the meantime, George Ephron had told Ives he needn't worry about the rent till he was on his feet, and the hotel was giving Ives his meals for a year's free subscription and a two-column ad.

He spent a troubled night, wakeful, trying to decide how he could appeal to Zachary. The next morning he ate breakfast early and came back to find Sabina sweeping out the office. He took the broom from her, smiling.

He said: "You've got to learn a few things if you're going to be a printer. These type slingers are notorious drunks. They're incurable travelers. If they get tired of a job in New York, they'll quit right in the middle of a run and the next week you'll see them in San Francisco. They're independent as a Missouri mule. They wouldn't be caught dead with anything but a composing stick in their hands. Such menial jobs as sweeping up are for the slaves, the untouchables, like copy boys."

"My goodness," she said. "They won't ever let me inside church again."

She was smiling, trying to match his mood. But there was a stiffness between them, an awkwardness. He knew it went back to the kiss yesterday, and what had been said. It had changed their relationship. He had a moment of doubt. He wondered if she would ever trust him. He wondered if a man ever really got to know this kind of a woman. She had lived with her family for eighteen years, and they didn't know her.

He held out his hand. "Sabina. . . ."

It was as far as he got. The puncheon walk outside shook to somebody's heavy tread and the door was pushed open. Zachary

Thayne stepped in. His face was grooved deeply with righteous anger.

"Git out of this place, Sabina," he said. "Hist yourself right back to the gap this minute. I come into town to look in on Eric and the first thing I hear . . . Sodom and Gomorrah . . . I didn't raise my girl to be no kept woman!"

Sabina turned scarlet. "Pa, it ain't no such thing. I been staying with Uncle Silas, same as usual. I just been helping Ives in the daytime."

"Daytime, nighttime, what's the difference? Anything could go on behind these locked doors."

"The door wasn't locked," Ives said. "The whole town can see through those windows. Why don't you quit treating Sabina like a child, Zachary? She's been a big help. I couldn't have gotten the paper out without her."

"Maybe better if you hadn't."

"You've seen my editorial."

"I seen your hogwash. Twenty Mile won't work, Ives. Nobody will go for it."

"Why not? Your land wouldn't have to be condemned, then. Medicine Lodge would stay as it is, untouched."

Zachary snorted. "Whose word have we got for that? Russell's? Once he got the rails to Twenty Mile, he'd bring them right on through."

"Why won't you trust Russell? He's gotten rid of Fargo. Doesn't that prove he's ready to compromise?"

"Fargo had to run. He's a wanted man. But that don't mean Russell's rid of him. He's still Russell's man. Russell ordered him to git Eric, the same as Russell ordered him to git Peter."

"It all began with Peter, didn't it?" Ives asked.

"It began with the railroad."

"I mean the real trouble . . . the real hate . . . it began when Peter was killed. Suppose it could be proved, once and for all, that nobody on Anchor did that. Would you be able to separate Fargo and Russell in your mind then?"

"Don't try to sidetrack me," Zachary said. He turned to Sabina, his eyes burning with his Biblical anger. "Are you coming back to the gap or do I have to drag you back?"

"You'll have to drag me back," she said. "And then you'll have to chain me up to keep me there, because if you don't, I'll run away. I'm a typesetter now, Pa. Typesetters are notorious drunks. They're incurable travelers. I could get a job anywhere in the world. You'll have to put a chain on me to keep me from it. Is that what you want the basin to know? How Zachary Thayne keeps his daughter chained up in the cabin same as one of his hounds?"

The gray-bearded man gaped at her. There was more bafflement than anger in his eyes now. Ives could hardly keep from smiling. He wondered if Zachary had ever met such defiance from his children before.

"Do you think Silas would let her come over here if he thought anything was wrong?" Ives asked. "Do you think the parson would? You'll just make yourself a laughingstock if you try to drag her out of here."

Zachary scowled uncertainly, pulling at his tangled gray beard. He was plainly at a loss. Maybe the biggest thing shaking him was the thought of appearing ridiculous before the town. But Peter Thayne was still on Ives's mind and he couldn't help going back to it, returning to the puzzle that had nagged at Ives ever since he had seen Sabina on Peter's Appaloosa.

"Zachary," he said, "you know about Tom Border hunting me. Suppose he came on Peter that day, at a distance . . . a man near my size, riding an Appaloosa . . . ?"

"Impossible," Zachary said. "Jeff Lee said this Border hit town the morning after you showed up, Ives. That means Border was a day behind you. Peter was killed the day before you came, two days before Border even hit the basin."

It was the piece that didn't fit, that had stymied Ives. Now he thought he had the key. It might have occurred to him sooner if the whole thing hadn't been pushed out of his mind by the violence of the last few days—Eric's beating, Jeff's death, his own smashed hands.

"Why do we keep assuming Border was behind me?" Ives said. "Just because he hit town after I did doesn't necessarily mean he reached the basin after I did. When I was leaving the basin that time, I made camp in the timber, off the road, where I was hidden. Border passed me during the night and went on to Twenty Mile. He could have done the same thing on the way in. There were a dozen places he could have passed me on the way from Rock Springs. A sandstorm came up the first day . . . blew me way off course. I spent the night in a sheep camp five miles east of the main trail."

Sabina was studying Ives curiously. She said wonderingly: "It could be. We found Peter's body not far from the gap. . . ."

"Hobble your jaw," Zachary told her. "A woman's mind ain't made for this kind of thinking. Border would've found out at the time that he'd killed the wrong man. Why should he wait two days before coming to town after you, Ives? It just doesn't fit. It was Fargo who killed Peter. You'll never prove different."

Zachary wheeled and stalked to the door. Ives thought his anger would make him forget what he had originally come for. With the door open, however, the towering man hesitated. He looked back at Sabina. He started to say something, checked himself, then muttered: "Well . . . not after dark, anyhow. You git back to your Uncle Silas before sundown."

"Yes, Pa," Sabina said meekly. Zachary still hesitated. He scowled at the floor, muttered something under his breath, and stamped out. Sabina grinned impishly at Ives. He couldn't help smiling back.

"What do you think about Peter?" he asked.

She sobered. "Does it matter?"

"I don't feel that way about a woman's mind, Sabina."

A grateful shine touched her eyes. "Well, I think you're right, Ives. It does go back to Peter. This idea, making Twenty Mile the shipping point . . . if somebody had thought of it before Peter was killed, Pa might have listened to reason."

"Then Tom Border's the key," Ives said.

"That bottleneck shell Doyle found near where Peter was shot," she said. "Would it fit Border's saddle gun?"

"I never got that close a look at it," he said. "But if it does. . . ."

"Border must be gone by now," she said.

"I thought so at first," Ives said. "Now I'm beginning to wonder. A man who'd hang on to hate this long, Sabina . . . he must have a fanatical streak in him. Would Doyle's threat be enough to scare him off? What if he's still in the basin, waiting for another chance at me?" Ives began to pace, the thought exciting him. "Silas is taking the Indian supplies north tomorrow. I could go with him. If I don't cut Border's sign before the Shoshone camp, I can pretty well count on them knowing whether he's still around. The Indians don't miss much that goes on in their country."

"Ives, you gave Doyle your word . . . you wouldn't get in a gunfight with Border again."

"I promised not in town," he said. "This won't be in town."

"That's splitting a mighty fine hair."

"It's got to be done."

"Then at least wait till Doyle gets back."

"He's gone after Fargo. It may be days. We can't afford to wait that long."

She came to him. She put her hands gently on his arms,

Les Savage, Jr.

looking at his bandaged hands. "You can't do it, Ives, not in this shape. . . ."

"I'm not so bad off. Doc Cabell says I'll be able to set type again."

"But not now. You can't even shoot a gun now."

"A man doesn't need fingers to shoot a gun. Border wouldn't be here if it hadn't been for me, Sabina. So much of this wouldn't have happened. I've got to make it right somehow."

She searched his face a moment more, as if hunting some final way to dissuade him. Then she made a hopeless little sound and moved into his arms. Her weight hung heavily against him. She kissed him and he could feel the tears on her cheeks.

"Ives," she said. "Why did I wait so long? I'm sure now. I'm just as sure as you are."

He held her tight, marveling at how soft and yielding a wild thing could be once it was caught. He kissed her again and buried his face in the corn-tassel shimmer of her hair.

"I wish I'd known this before," he said. "I would have gone after Border a lot sooner."

She pulled back. "If you insist on going, I'll go with you."

"Now hold on, Sabina . . . a girl . . . it would be too dangerous."

She tossed her head angrily. With that quicksilver change of mood she was once more a hoyden, a broomtail never touched by the halter. "You can't stop me. I'll borrow a horse from Ephron. Uncle Silas, he can give me a pair of jeans."

He felt frustrated. He could understand the baffled look in Zachary's eyes now. He thought of hog-tying her, but that seemed silly.

"All right," he said. "But you better get to bed early. Silas is leaving at dawn."

Her eyes danced triumphantly. "I been getting up at dawn for eighteen years."

170

XVIII

That evening, after Ives was sure Sabina had gone to bed, he crossed to the general store and knocked softly on the kitchen door. Silas was dozing in his big chair, untouched ledgers in his lap. The tapping finally woke him and he came outside. In a low voice Ives told the man his problem. Silas said the wagon was already loaded and they could start that night. They'd be a day's ride away from Sabina by the time she woke up. It would discourage her, and she would probably be hurt enough at Ives so she wouldn't try to follow. By the time they got back she'd be over her mad.

Ives went back for his horse and his arms. Ives's splinted fingers were too stiff and too thickly bandaged to work the trigger on his gun, so Silas tied them back, enabling him to fire the gun by slapping the hammer with the heel of his hand.

Another mule train had come through the gap with the supplies and the storekeeper had borrowed a heavy Espinshied freight wagon from Ephron, hauled by four of the biggest horses in town. Ives hitched his Appaloosa behind and rode the high front seat. About 3:00 in the morning they reached the Anchor roundup camp. They slept there till dawn, and then dumped enough grub for three or four days.

The crew ate like a bunch of schoolboys at a picnic and Sowbelly even smiled once. But Ives could see how badly they missed Fargo. The horses were galled and gaunted from overwork; the gather was still notably thin. Parson had tried to take Fargo's place. He freely admitted his failure.

"You don't really appreciate a man's stripe till you try to fill his boots," he said. "I never really knew what Fargo was contendin' with . . . short of grub, short of horses, short of men. Kendricks and Quill quit after that mess with Tom Russell, you know. Even that new hand didn't come back."

"What new hand?" Ives asked.

171

"Never did say his name. Showed up the same night Russell was hurt. Big jasper, hair the color of new rope. . . ."

"Claybank horse? Corkscrew brand?"

"That's right."

"Tom Border," Silas said.

It took Ives a moment to digest. Then a new thought struck him. "Could Border have known Kendricks and Quill were going after Silas's wagon at Long Grade?" Ives asked. "Could Border have known I was aboard?"

"Kendricks had a big ruckus with Fargo about it that evening," Parson said. "Your name was mentioned. Could be Border overheard."

Ives looked at Silas. "You want to lay a bet?"

"I'm 'way ahead of you," Silas said. "It was Tom Border that shot at you on Long Grade."

They were all silent for a moment, and then Hoback shook his head sadly. "Well . . . that don't help Fargo much now."

"Doyle figured Fargo would be heading for the Indian country," Ives said.

"Doyle was by here," Hoback said. "But you won't find him in the Indian country. He headed west, toward Sheeptown. Seems he heard Fargo was over there."

"Where'd he hear that?" Ives asked.

Hoback didn't answer. Slowly his head turned till he was looking at Parson. The rest of the crew was looking at the black-bearded man, too. Parson stopped eating. His head lowered till his beard spread against his chest, and his hat brim hid his eyes.

"Judas," he said. "Betrayest thou the Son of Man with a kiss?"

Ives and Silas left the roundup camp shortly after sunup. They were north of the river now, a wild primitive area, and they went all day without any sign of a human being. The wagon road petered out to a rough travois trail and later to a game trace. It was a battle to move the wagon and sometimes Ives had to hitch a rope on the outfit and help pull with his Appaloosa. They reached the Indian camp near dusk, twenty or thirty skin lodges scattered across a buffalo-grass meadow. The wind was changing as the wagon entered the clearing. Ives could hear a lot of coughing from within the teepees and the old squaws were hopping around outside and opening the smoke flaps on the downwind side to suck the smoke out.

Silas told Ives: "They're Shoshones, I guess, but we call 'em Sheep Eaters. Used to live in Yellowstone, hunt them bighorns up there. I've had this supply contract for twenty years and I still don't know if they're just bein' ornery or if they're really too dumb to learn English."

As the wagon pulled to a halt in the clearing, the Indians began to gather around it. Their black hair was long and dirty, braided with strips of yarn or colored cloth. Their buckskins were worn so thin they had a satiny shine and gave off the smell of smoke that never seemed to leave squaw-tanned hide. Silas pointed out the headmen. One of them was named Two Kettle and his chest was marked by two puckered sun-dance scars. While the Indians were unloading the wagon, Silas made sign talk with Two Kettle. The Indian took a long time answering, waving his arms and slapping his chest and making various signals with his fingers.

"He says they don't know anything about Tom Border," Silas told Ives. "But there are some hunting parties out in the Barricades south of here. If Border's in the mountains, they might have cut his sign."

Two Kettle made a ceremonious gesture toward one of the lodges and Silas said they were going to hold council and get something to eat. Ives looked around the camp as they started for the lodge. On the far side of camp he caught sight of a horse that had been hidden before. It was hitched to a rope line beside one of the outlying lodges. It was Fargo's tiger-striped roan.

Ives stopped, his bandaged hand going impulsively to his holstered gun. Silas saw what he was looking at and said sharply: "Hold it, Ives. It ain't that easy."

Ives didn't draw his gun. He realized what Silas meant. The Indians had pulled away, their faces masked, hostile. A sullen murmur ran through their crowd. A young buck appeared at the door of a lodge, a Winchester in his hands.

"Ask them where Fargo is," Ives said. "Tell them he's a wanted man . . . he killed Jeff Lee."

Silas made sign talk again. Ives was searching the camp nervously for some other sign of Fargo. The Indians began talking among themselves in Shoshone, apparently having an argument. Then Two Kettle turned to Silas and began using his hands again. Silas translated for Ives.

"Two Kettle says some of the Indians who ran with Kelly Fargo eighteen years ago are still around. They were for letting Fargo stay. But Two Kettle and the headmen don't like it. They don't want no more trouble. Kelly Fargo brought them enough grief before. They don't want the U.S. Army on their necks again."

"Then where is Fargo?"

Silas didn't get a chance to ask. Two Kettle was already starting toward the lodge near Fargo's roan. Ives and Silas and a file of Indians trailed him. Ives pulled his gun. Two Kettle stopped before the lodge, pulling the door flap back. He did not enter, and was apparently waiting for the white man. They both hesitated.

Finally Silas said: "I don't think Two Kettle would slip us a cold deck."

He started toward the door. Ives accompanied him, the gun held ready. They had to stoop to peer inside. Ives's eyes took a moment to adjust. He saw the Indian girl sitting beside the circle of rocks that contained the dead ashes of a fire. She wore a buckskin dress hung with elks' teeth. She was braiding her hair and she looked at Ives without stopping. Her eyes were veiled, remote.

Beyond her, sprawled on his back on a buffalo robe, lay Fargo. All he had on were his jeans. He was barefoot and shirtless, and his body was startlingly white against the swart buffalo hide. It was a body lean to the point of gauntness, with a big rib cage like a runner's, and muscles that had a stringy hardness even in relaxation. It made Ives think of a hungry wolf. The reek of liquor hung so heavily in the closed air of the lodge that it brought tears to Ives's eyes.

"That's *tiswin*," Silas said. "The Indians make it from corn. I never knew Fargo to throw a drunk before."

The talk didn't wake Fargo. His beard stubble was an inch long, matted with burrs and dirt. It gave him a ragged, beggar's face. His mouth was open and he was snoring softly. There was something vulnerable about his whole position. Ives knew he should hate the man for killing Jeff Lee. But in that moment Fargo only looked pathetic.

Ives stepped inside. Two Kettle said something and the girl rose, drifting out like a shadow. Ives toed Fargo. He had to shove hard before the man stirred.

Fargo groaned and opened his bloodshot eyes. They were blank for a moment. Then they focused on Ives. Fargo grunted and sat up with startling speed. Ives shoved the gun in his face. Fargo stared at it, the creases of strain dug deep beneath his jaw. Finally he settled back. He closed his eyes and wiped a hand across his mouth.

"Well," he said huskily. "It's what everybody expected, ain't it?"

"Doyle has a warrant out for you," Ives said. "You'd better get your clothes on and we'll take you back."

Fargo opened his eyes again, looking malevolently at Ives. "Nobody's taking me back."

"I'm thinking of Jeff Lee," Ives said. "Either you get dressed, Fargo . . . or you get hit on the head and dumped in the wagon just as naked as you sit there now."

Silas and Ives didn't want to stay among the Shoshones with their prisoner. They were afraid that some of the renegades who had ridden with Fargo's father might try to set Fargo free. They pulled out of camp as soon as the wagon was unloaded, with Fargo sitting between Ives and the older man, his hands tied behind him with rawhide. Ives still couldn't forget Border. He remembered Two Kettle mentioning the hunting parties in the Barricades. Silas told him about a different route back that would take them through the mountains. It would take a lot longer but Ives asked him to follow it, hoping they would run into some of the hunters.

They drove till midnight and made a fireless camp in a grove of aspens. Silas rolled into his blankets under the wagon while Ives took the first watch. He was groggy from the long day and stayed on his feet to keep awake. Fargo sat against the wagon wheel, hands still tied behind him. Starlight cast the man's face in black shadow beneath his hat.

"I think Parson sent Doyle on a wild-goose chase," Ives said. "He told Doyle you'd been seen in Sheeptown."

"Trust Parson," Fargo said cynically. "A last favor for a friend."

Ives wondered if Parson had done it for Fargo—or for Russell. "Maybe your crew thought more of you than you realize," Ives said.

"I'm Kelly Fargo's son. That's all they thought of me. That's all anybody thought of me. And now Tom Russell."

"He gave you all the rope he could, Fargo."

"No he didn't. He read your editorial. That's what he did."

"Russell would've had to face this sooner or later."

"We could've worked it out . . . without you. Maybe you cut my rope, Ives, but I won't let you cut Tom's, too."

"I haven't got anything against Tom Russell."

"What do you think will happen to him without me?" Fargo asked. "He's helpless now. The Thaynes, the town, the whole basin . . . they'll go for him. They think they got him now. They think they'll smash him."

"Is that why you didn't leave the basin?"

"They won't pull him down, Ives. Not while I'm alive. They been waiting for this all my life. They wanted Kelly Fargo back? Well, now they've got him."

Ives saw there was no use talking any more. Something had left Fargo. The humanity he had seen in the man, had been able to touch at times, seemed gone. He wondered if he had ever really touched it, or why he had tried. He thought of Jeff Lee and his throat closed up. He had fought against it—but in that moment he hated Fargo. He wondered if the basin wasn't right, if Fargo hadn't really inherited his father's evil. And yet Fargo was still defending Russell, was loyal to him, even though the man had rejected Fargo. Why were some of a man's actions so reasonable and others so senseless? It made him think of what Jeff had talked about—thinking and feeling, the eternal conflict between passion and logic in a man. And loyalty could be a passion, as well as hate.

Fargo finally fell asleep against the wheel. Ives waked Silas when the stars faded. Silas carried no short gun but he had a Winchester he kept in the wagon.

"Watch him close, and don't get within reach of him," Ives told Silas.

The pudgy man frowned at Fargo. "It makes me spooky, Ives. The way he was watching you . . . all the way down from the

Shoshone camp."

"That Indian *tiswin*'s still firing him up," Ives said.

He had a few hours' uneasy sleep before Silas woke him at sunup. They had a meal of bacon and coffee and hardtack, and rolled the wagon. They were still in Shoshone country. During the forenoon they met two hunting parties. Ives asked about Border but none of the Indians had seen him. Then, in mid-afternoon, they reached Wind River and ran into a group of Indians. There were three of them, with the carcass of an elk slung across their spare horse. They said they had made the kill at the head of the river. Ives asked about Border. They said they had seen a man in camp near the headwaters, about three hours away, a man in a yellow sheepskin, with a claybank horse.

Ives had pitted himself against Border's moves for so long that he almost knew what had gone on in the man's mind when Border had been unable to find Ives's body in the wreckage of the wagon at Long Grade. Border had known he couldn't stay at the Anchor roundup camp much longer without their finding out who he was. He had decided to pull back into the mountains and bide his time until he found out what had happened to Ives.

"Let's take Fargo to town first," Silas said. "Doyle will be back by now."

"We've got Border pretty well pinpointed," Ives said. "Put it off and we'd have the whole basin to scour again."

"Then let me go with you. We can take Fargo."

"You'd still have your hands full watching him. It would be better for one of us, without anything to worry about behind him. It's my job, Silas. It's been my job from the first."

Ives still hesitated, and Silas must have guessed what was on his mind. The little storekeeper bristled. "I'll be all right. Zachary and me had to fight the Indians for this basin."

Ives grinned and clapped him on the shoulder. He gave a last glance at Fargo, then turned to unhitch his Appaloosa and swing aboard. He headed the horse upstream.

Fargo watched Ives till he was out of sight. The hate must have showed in his face, because Silas shook his head disgustedly.

"Why don't you spit that poison where it belongs?" Silas said. "Ives was still trying to give you the benefit of the doubt when every other soul in this basin had turned ag'in' you. If you want to blame anybody for your trouble, you oughtta blame this Tom Border. Ives thinks it was him killed Peter Thayne."

Fargo didn't answer. His head still throbbed with the hangover from the *tiswin*. He felt sick to his stomach and all he could think of was Ives. It seemed as though all the pain he had suffered from the basin was now focused in Ives.

"Was it you shot at Ives at Long Grade?" Silas said.

Fargo could remain silent no longer. "I give my word there wouldn't be no more trouble. You think I'd break my word to Tom Russell?"

"Then it must've been Tom Border," Silas said. "It was Tom Border that caused Russell's legs to be smashed, Fargo. It was Tom Border that hurt Russell, not Ives. Can't you git that through your head?"

It didn't make much impression on Fargo. There was a fog on his mind. It had been there ever since he had left Anchor for the last time. About all he could remember of that night was his savage impulse to get Ives. Why hadn't it lasted? Why hadn't he gone after Ives? Maybe it had been the sickness in him—the knowledge that Russell had finally rejected him—smothering everything else in his mind, taking the strength out of him, the feelings, the will. He supposed it was natural, in such a state, for him to drift north during that lost time. The Shoshone camp was a logical place for the son of Kelly Fargo to end up.

He realized that Silas had stopped talking to him. The man

had gathered some wood for a fire and put the coffee pot on. Fargo studied the paunchy little storekeeper squatting by the fire, thinking how Silas was another one who had always given him the benefit of the doubt. Who had always tried to give him a chance. Kind-hearted. Today it was going to be his weakness.

When the coffee was done, Silas poured a cup, and Fargo said: "You gonna keep it all to yourself?"

Silas glanced at him, hesitated, then brought the cup over. He held it to Fargo's lips, keeping the gun tucked under one arm all the time. Fargo didn't make his move till the cup was empty. It was then that Silas rose and turned to go back toward the fire. For that instant his back was turned to Fargo and he was still within reach.

Fargo threw himself bodily at Silas. He struck the man back of the knees with all his weight. It buckled the storekeeper's legs and he pitched forward on his face. Silas grunted heavily and tried to roll over, fumbling to retrieve his dropped Winchester. But Fargo was already up. He jumped Silas and kicked viciously at his head. The toe of his boot caught the man at the temple. Fargo kicked again, as hard as he could. But the first one had done the job, and the second kick only made Silas's inert body jerk slackly.

Quickly Fargo circled the wagon until he found a bolt with its threading extending an inch beyond the nut. He stood with his back to it and began scraping his rawhide lashings back and forth across the threads. Before they had frayed the rawhide enough to break, his hands and wrists were torn and bleeding. When he was free, he crossed and picked up the Winchester. They had hitched his roan behind the wagon and he untied it and swung into the saddle. Silas was beginning to stir feebly, as Fargo rode out. The prints of Ives's horse were clearly visible in the muck along the creekbank.

Fargo followed them.

XIX

For most of the afternoon Ives had followed Wind River up into the Barricades. He kept to the deep timber bordering the river, moving cautiously, covering himself. He had begun to realize how blindly he had gone after Border, only thinking in terms of finding the man, getting to him. There was more to it than that. What if the bottleneck cartridge did fit Border's saddle gun? Would it be conclusive enough evidence that Border had killed Peter Thayne? Would it convince Zachary? Ives knew Zachary's blindness. He was afraid it wouldn't be enough. And with the fear came the realization that he would need something more. Border had to talk. The only way he could be certain would be to take Border alive.

The sun was low when Ives reached snow line. He began passing drifts that filled the coulées and stood a foot deep in timber. Black lichen covered the lodgepole trunks, hoary as an old man's beard. He had to pass through a few thin spots, and, when he did, he always halted at the edge of the heavy timber, studying the opening ahead carefully, before he exposed himself. Every hundred yards or so he stopped anyway, searching all about him for some sign. If he hadn't been so careful, he wouldn't have seen the movement behind him.

It was during one of his halts, and his eye was caught by a shadowy flutter far down the slope. He waited, and in a moment a rider appeared, entering one of the same open patches Ives had crossed. Ives saw the black hat, the yellow gloves, and knew it was Fargo, following his tracks.

He could guess what had happened to Silas, and it filled him with bitter outrage. But it was obvious what Fargo had come for. Ives knew he couldn't stop to fight the man. If Border was anywhere nearby, the first gunshot would warn him. Ives had to get to Border first.

He moved faster, discarding some of his caution. He was

blocked by a big chokecherry thicket and lost precious time skirting the miniature jungle, not wanting to give himself away popping brush. A wind had risen, booming through the timber. It lifted the hard-packed snow and whipped it against Ives in buckshot blasts. He had remained deep enough in timber so that he couldn't be seen from the river, but he could hear its boiling roar on his right flank whenever the wind died.

His sense of urgency was like a pressure building up against him. He knew he didn't have much more time. Fargo would catch up with him soon. But it would be too dangerous to move any faster. It was too easy to miss sign. It was too easy to come on a camp unexpectedly in the timber.

He was a hundred yards upslope from the cherry thicket when he caught sight of the smoke, shredded by the wind and fading against the sky almost as soon as it emerged from the tree tops. He judged it to come from a fire on the opposite bank of the river.

He dismounted, tightening the Appaloosa's noseband so she wouldn't betray him by whinnying. He was reaching to pull his saddle gun from its scabbard when a crashing sound came from the cherry thicket downslope. It startled the skittish mare. She shied, reared, and started to bolt. Ives made a lunge for her but he missed the reins and it only made her spook more wildly.

What he saw in the thicket kept him from running after the Appaloosa. It was Fargo, still busting brush as he forced his horse uphill through the chokecherry.

Knowing the man had seen him, Ives wheeled and plunged into the dense timber toward the river. He was hidden in the trees before Fargo could get close enough for a shot. Ives reached the river, clinging to the hope that Border hadn't heard the popping brush over the roar of the water.

He slid down the miniature cliff of the riverbank, pulling his gun. It was a big Paterson five-shot his father had used during the war. It felt clumsy in his bandaged hands, awkward.

The river was narrow here near headwaters, rimed with ice at the edges, tumbling and foaming over the stones that choked its course. Ives plunged across in half a dozen steps, the icy water boiling over his knees. The opposite bank was a steep incline of shale and sand, slippery with pine needles.

He lunged toward the top, knowing he only had a few moments left, still hoping the river would cover his noise. He saw a scatter of rocks at the top and squirmed into them for cover. He could see that he was on the edge of a high park but a big deadfall lay about ten feet from the rocks, blocking his view. He crawled to the rotten, fallen tree on his belly and peered over the top.

The camp was startlingly near, no more than two hundred feet away. The steep slant of the meadow was studded with moss-blackened boulders, and beyond them stood the unsaddled claybank, hitched to a tree, with the saddle and other gear scattered around a smoking fire. Tom Border was crouched near the flames, spitting a venison steak. He was faced toward Ives, but his head was down.

Ives rose, his gun on Border. He started to move in—when he heard Fargo charge out of the timber across the river. Ives couldn't help wheeling to look. Fargo had come on the river unexpectedly, running his horse so hard that he couldn't pull up in time. The roan went off the edge and slid down the steep bank. Ives saw Fargo pitch out of the saddle and the horse emitted a whinnying scream as it crashed into the rocks of the streambed.

Ives whirled back toward Border. The man had already reacted to the sound. His head had snapped up and he was staring blankly at Ives. He dropped the steak and lunged for his rifle, lying against the saddle a foot away.

"Border!" Ives shouted. "You don't stand a chance!"

Border already had his gun, snapping down the loading lever. His eyes were glittering, fanatical, and he had started running at Ives. All Ives could do was start fanning.

Every time he hit the hammer with the heel of his bandaged hand the Paterson kicked a little, and Ives knew it was playing hell with his aim. Border's first try was a snap shot, from the hip, while he was running forward. Ives heard it slam into the deadfall at his feet.

One of Ives's bullets struck home as Border snapped his loading lever down. It jarred Border and made him stumble. For a moment Ives thought he was going down. But Border caught himself, stumbling on. He shambled loosely toward Ives, his eyes glassy, his mouth twisted with strain. He was trying to get his gun raised again, as though it were an enormous weight.

Ives fanned his gun again. He saw the bullet drive into Border. The man seemed to stop, for a moment, and then stumbled on. Ives kept on slapping his hammer till it snapped on an empty chamber.

Border came on another pair of steps, still trying to get his gun up. Then he fell into the heap of moss-black boulders, and his gun went off at the ground.

Ives heard a scrambling sound from the riverbank behind him and realized it was Fargo coming up. Cursing a gun that only held five bullets, he crawled across the deadfall and sprawled behind it on the other side. He started trying to get a cartridge from its belt loop with his clumsy, bandaged fingers. He had the shell out when he heard Fargo scramble over the edge of the riverbank.

His stiff fingers fumbled the shell, dropping it. He knew he would never be in time. He heard Fargo's pounding feet just beyond the deadfall. He rose up from behind the tree, saw the man not four feet away, soaking wet, and heaved his empty gun.

Fargo's eyes were blank with complete surprise. It was what

betrayed him. He was trying to swing his Winchester around toward Ives when the heavy Paterson hit him in the face. He made a broken sound and almost fell, so stunned by the blow that he couldn't stop running. He lunged into the fallen tree trunk, sprawling across its waist-high barrier of branches and foliage. Ives caught the Winchester in both bandaged hands, tearing it out of Fargo's grip.

Fargo straightened up. He put his hands to his bleeding face for a moment. He was fighting for breath, from the run, and sweat made a greasy shine on his sharp cheeks. Ives heard another sound down in the riverbed and in a moment Silas toiled up over the edge. He stopped, breathing so heavily that he couldn't speak for a moment. "I'm sorry," he told Ives. "Fargo got the drop on me. I cut a horse out of the team, followed his sign."

Ives didn't answer. He turned to look at the spot where Border had fallen. Silas must have guessed what was on his mind. The storekeeper crossed to where one of Border's empty shells lay on the ground, ejected by the action of the saddle gun. Silas picked it up. Ives saw that it was copper-cased, bottleneck, the same kind of shell Doyle had found near Peter Thayne's body.

Ives was startled by a feeble stirring from Border. The rocks in which the man lay hid most of him and apparently prevented him from seeing Ives.

"Whattayou gabbing about?" Border said. His voice was husky, far away. "Where's Ives? Did that last shot git him?"

Silas started to answer, but Ives made a quick motion with one hand to stop him. It struck Ives that, if Border thought he had failed to kill Ives, he might refuse to tell anything, out of sheer malice. Ives nodded his head up and down emphatically, and Silas seemed to get the idea.

"Ives is dead," Silas told Border. "You got him."

Border started to laugh. It made him choke and go into a weak paroxysm of coughing. Ives pointed silently at the bottleneck shell in Silas's hand.

"What about Peter Thayne?" Silas asked Border.

Border tried to stop coughing. "Who's Peter Thayne?"

"The boy on the Appaloosa that you shot near the gap."

"I never seen him."

Silas crouched down beside the man. "You might as well talk, Border. Your light's going out fast." Border didn't answer, and finally Silas said, in a deliberately goading voice: "I thought not. Peter was pretty fast with a gun. You wouldn't have the guts to go against him."

"The hell I wouldn't. He was just a kid."

"How did you happen onto him?"

"Met some Indians . . . this end of the gap. Sign talk. Asked about Ives. They said . . . seen a man . . . Appaloosa . . . coupla hours off. Running a herd of bronc's." Border choked again, his voice growing fainter. "Near dark when I found him . . . come on him sudden. He must've thought I was Anchor . . . pulled his gun. I was certain he was Ives then . . . shot before I was close enough to see . . . mistake. . . ."

"That was two days before you hit town. Why did you wait so long?"

"Didn't wanna be strung up for killing the wrong man. Hung around near the gap . . . coupla days, run into some farmers coming from the funeral. They said everybody blamed Fargo for the killing . . . I knew I was in the clear then. Went . . . hunting Ives . . . Ives. . . ."

Border ended with a sighing sound. Silas rose slowly, and Ives knew Border was dead. Fargo was staring at the rocks. Something had happened to his face; it had gone loose around the mouth, and the baleful light was gone from his eyes. They looked glazed, empty of life. He walked to a lower part of the deadfall and sat down. He wiped the back of his hand across his mouth. His shoulders bowed and he closed his eyes and let all the breath out of him in a long wheezing sound. Ives didn't think he had ever seen such complete defeat in a man. He couldn't feel hate for Fargo any more. He couldn't feel pity, either. He only knew that Fargo would have to pay for Jeff. Ives still believed Fargo had not intended to kill Jeff, and knew he would have to testify to that. It would probably be manslaughter for Fargo. Maybe one to ten in the state penitentiary. Ives doubted if Fargo would try to come back when he was out. It would be better that way.

Ives spoke to Silas: "Will Zachary believe you about Border?"

"Zachary knows I wouldn't lie to him," Silas said. "It's going to make a difference, Ives. I think we'll be able to git Zachary and Russell together now. I think it'll give us all a new start."

Ives was thinking about Audrey and Eric, and how much they needed the new start. He was thinking about Sabina. He was swept with a sudden impatience to get back to her, to see her. He had been away too long.

"Let's get the horses, Silas," he said. "My type slinger will give me hell if I'm late for the Wednesday edition."

ABOUT THE AUTHOR

Les Savage, Jr. was born in Alhambra, California and grew up in Los Angeles. His first published story was "Bullets and Bull-whips" accepted by the prestigious magazine, Street & Smith's *Western Story*. Almost ninety more magazine stories followed, all set on the American frontier, many of them published in Fiction House magazines such as *Frontier Stories* and *Lariat Story Magazine* where Savage became a superstar with his name on many covers. His first novel, *Treasure of the Brasada*, appeared from Simon & Schuster in 1947. Due to his preference for historical accuracy, Savage often ran into problems with book editors in the 1950s who were concerned about marriages between his protagonists and women of different races—a commonplace on the real frontier but not in much Western fiction in that decade. Savage died young, at thirty-five, from complications arising out of hereditary diabetes and elevated cholesterol. However, as a result of the censorship imposed on many of his works, only now are they being fully restored by returning to the author's original manuscripts. Among Savage's finest Western stories are *Fire Dance at Spider Rock* (Five Star Westerns, 1995), *Medicine Wheel* (Five Star Westerns, 1996), *Coffin Gap* (Five Star Westerns, 1997), *Phantoms in the Night* (Five Star Westerns, 1998), *The Bloody Quarter* (Five Star Westerns, 1999), *In The Land of Little Sticks* (Five Star Westerns, 2000), *The Cavan Breed* (Five Star Westerns, 2001), and *Danger Rides the River* (Five Star Westerns, 2002), *Black Rock Cañon*

(Five Star Westerns, 2006). Much as Stephen Crane before him, while he wrote, the shadow of his imminent death grew longer and longer across his young life, and he knew that, if he was going to do it at all, he would have to do it quickly. He did it well, and, now that his novels and stories are being restored to what he had intended them to be, his achievement irradiated by his powerful and profoundly sensitive imagination will be with us always, as he had wanted it to be, as he had so rushed against time and mortality that it might be. *Outlaws of the Brasada* will be his next Five Star Western.